**WINNER OF THE
CRIMEFEST AWARD FOR
BEST CRIME NOVEL
FOR CHILDREN 2021**

SAINSBURY'S
**CHILDREN'S BOOK
AWARDS 2021**

PRAISE FOR *TWITCH*

"Leonard knows her audience and the jeopardy comes
in flocks… Find your nest, curl up and enjoy."
THE TIMES, CHILDREN'S BOOK OF THE WEEK

"A twist-laden, thriller-like tale."
OBSERVER

"A lively, twisty crime drama as well as a persuasive
story about friendship and protecting nature."
SUNDAY TIMES

"Another soaring success from Leonard."
DAILY MAIL

"A tale of friendship, of being yourself, of seeking
solace in nature … simply genius."
BBC WILDLIFE

"[A] pacy mystery adventure."
iNEWSPAPER

"A superb adventure of friendship, bravery
and the wonderful world of birds."
THE BOOKSELLER

"One of those really, really good books!"
THE BOOKBAG

"Leonard has crafted an intelligent mystery
from unlikely material, with bonus bird facts."
IRISH TIMES

SPARK

M. G. LEONARD

WALKER
BOOKS

First published 2022 by Walker Books Ltd
87 Vauxhall Walk, London SE11 5HJ

2 4 6 8 10 9 7 5 3 1

Text © 2022 MG Leonard Ltd.
Cover illustrations © 2022 Paddy Donnelly
Map illustrations © 2022 Laurissa Jones

The right of M. G. Leonard to be identified as author of
this work has been asserted in accordance with
the Copyright, Designs and Patents Act 1988

This book has been typeset in Berkeley and Futura

Printed and bound by CPI Group (UK) Ltd, Croydon CR0 4YY

British Library Cataloguing in Publication Data:
a catalogue record for this book is available from the British Library

ISBN 978-1-4063-8938-8

www.walker.co.uk

For Arthur, with love.

"Vultures are the most righteous
of birds: they do not attack even
the smallest living creature."
—Plutarch

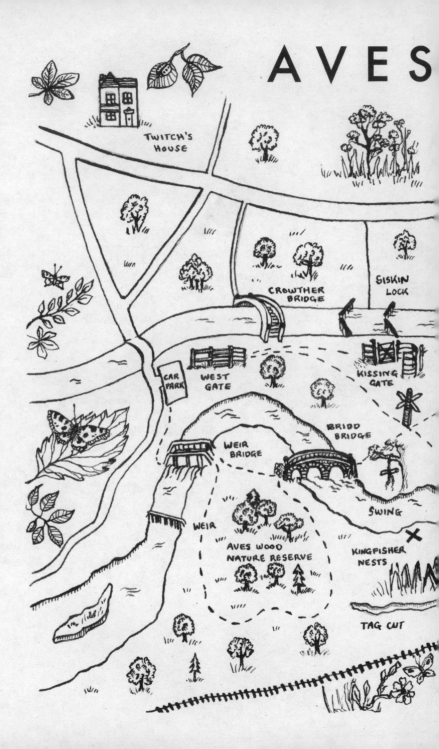

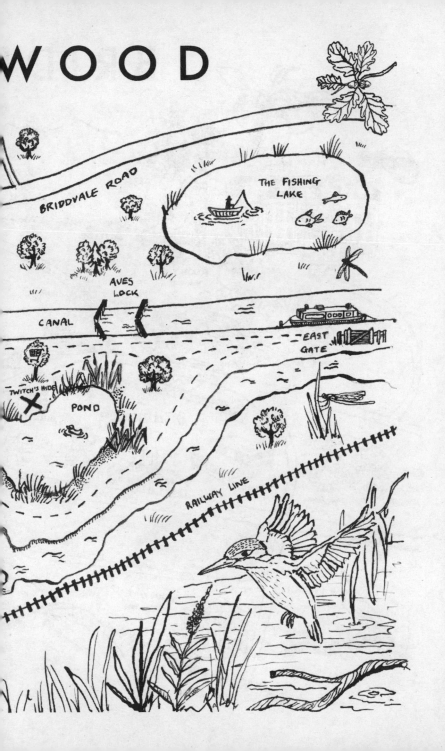

BRIDD

STABLES

MORD HALL

GROUSE
MOOR

GAMEKEEPER'S
COTTAGE

ROOKY
WOOD

TOWN
HALL

CHURCH

TWI

HIGH STREET

PLAYGROUND

BRIDDVALE

TERRY

THE OLD
MILL

OZURU

VET

SCHOOL

CANAL

TARA

BRIDDVALE
STATION

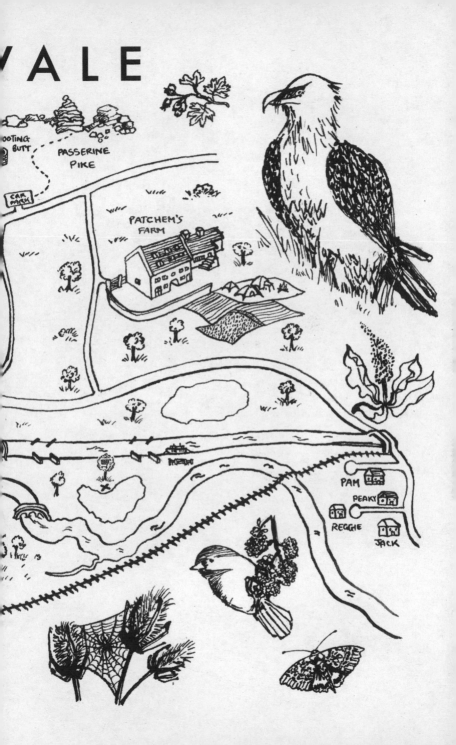

VALE

SHOOTING
BUTT

PASSERINE
PIKE

CAR
PARK

PATCHEM'S
FARM

PAM

PEAKY

REGGIE

JACK

1

ZOMBIE

A soul-chilling howl paralysed Jack as he entered
Aves Wood. The hairs on his body lifted as a scream
reverberated through the trees. It was a horrible sound,
writhing with tones of fear, pain and agony. It sent birds
bolting skywards, seeking safety in the clouds.

Alarmed, Jack cautiously peered along the path,
scouring the browning bracken beyond the east gate
for any sign of a monstrous hell hound. Without taking
his eyes from the path, he bent down and picked up
a stick that was lying on the ground.

What had made that unearthly noise?

Jack felt like he was stepping into one of his own
fantasies. In his most frequent daydream, a dangerous
dishevelled army of the undead would hunt his friends
across an apocalyptic landscape, desperate to dine on
their flesh. Twitch, Ozuru, Ava, Tippi, Terry and Tara

would get trapped with their backs to a wall. They'd be about to have their limbs torn off and gnawed on, like barbecued chicken wings, when Jack, seeing his friends in danger, would vault over the wall, dropping down in front of them in a superhero pose. Armed only with a golf club, he would fight the flesh-eating zombies, defeating them in a gruesome battle, and saving his friends.

At least I'm wearing my boots, combats and camo coat, he thought. I can always run and hide. He raised the stick high above his head, wishing it was a metal golf club.

"Here, Zombie, Zombie," he called softly, creeping forward. "Come out, come out, wherever you are." He approached a clump of ferns beneath an old oak tree. Something was in there; he could sense it. "Let's make a deal, I won't decapitate you, if you don't bite me."

The reply was a vicious noise, like fat crackling in a wet frying pan, followed by another banshee scream.

Warily, Jack parted the fan of decaying ferns with his stick, jumping backwards as his ears were assaulted by a harrowing shriek. Just for a second, he had glimpsed the shocking sight of a ginger cat, eyes wide, ears flat against its head, blood all over its haunches.

"Not a zombie then," Jack said to himself, trying to calm his hammering heart. He sat down on the ground in front of the cat's hiding place. The undergrowth vibrated with a low growl of warning. Zombie cat wasn't going to let anyone touch it.

What should he do? The cat needed help, he could see that. Should he go to the hide, where his friends were meeting to plan the half-term holiday? It would take at least twenty minutes to bring them back here. In that time Zombie cat might move, or whatever attacked it might come back to finish it off.

Jack wished Twitch were here. He was Jack's best friend and leader of the Twitchers, their birdwatching squad. He was brilliant at handling animals, even cats, which he didn't like because they killed birds.

What would Twitch do? Instinctively, Jack knew the answer. Twitch would get the hurt cat to a vet as quickly as he could, even if it meant he got bitten, scratched and missed the meeting with his friends.

"OK, Zombie," Jack said softly. "You're going to have to trust me." He put the stick down, as a gentle wind rustled the golden leaves above him. Rising to his knees, he parted the ferns with his hands. The cat howled and spat, baring its teeth, hunkering down as if it were going to pounce.

Ignoring the noise, Jack peered at the cat's injury, grimacing at the sight of fur matted with congealed blood. The cat's left hind leg was hanging at an odd angle. It couldn't have run away from him even if it wanted to. He studied the poor moggy. It didn't look like it had been in a fight. There were no claw marks or any other injuries. And it couldn't have been hit by a car: they were too far from the road. A trail of flattened plants showed the way the cat had dragged itself into this hiding place. It must've been hurt in Aves Wood, but by what … or who?

If he left the cat here, Jack feared it would die.

There was a vet on the Briddvale Road, about a mile away, outside town. Could he get the cat there? Hoping to spot something or someone useful, Jack looked around. He saw glossy hawthorn berries dangling from lichen-covered branches, butterflies and buzzing beasties feeding on overripe crab apples, but he couldn't see anything that would help him carry a petrified injured cat.

Twitch had taught him that the key to dealing with frightened animals was to be calm, firm, gentle and swift. Wriggling out of his camo anorak, Jack pulled off his grey hoodie and put his coat back on, taking his gloves from his pockets. He tucked the hoodie into the neck of his coat, spreading the jumper across his chest, and pulled his gloves on. His heart was hopping about nervously.

Closing his eyes, he inhaled the calming earthy scent of autumn. He could do this.

"OK, Zombie, I'm going to pick you up now." Jack flattened the ferns and Zombie shrank into a defensive posture, snarling at him. "Please don't attack me, Zombie. I'm trying to help." His words had no effect on the distressed cat. "Oh yikes," he muttered to himself. "This is going to hurt."

Before he could overthink, Jack leaned forwards, placing his hands around the cat's middle, careful not to touch its injured hindquarters. He lifted it, swiftly, hugging its head and front half under his right armpit, keeping the injured end of the animal up.

The cat clawed at him, wildly. Jack's coat and hoodie protected his ribs, but he sucked in air as one of Zombie's razor-sharp talons caught him across the forearm, raking his skin.

A sickening waft of poop told him that the cat had soiled itself, and a wave of nausea turned Jack's stomach, but he didn't have time to worry because Zombie was wriggling and spitting, trying to escape.

"It's all right, Zombie," Jack said, struggling to keep hold of the cat. He manoeuvred his right arm so that it pinned the cat against him, and, using his teeth, he freed the hoodie from the neck of his coat, letting it drop over the cat's head, so that it enveloped the feline and hid the world. He kept its injured backside lifted, touching nothing.

Jack stared at the cat's thigh, which was oozing blood. He could see a hole. Was it made by a bullet? Had someone shot Zombie? He was horrified. Who would do a thing like that?

Rising to his feet, Jack half walked, half jogged, with bent knees, moving as smoothly and swiftly as possible along the familiar paths of Aves Wood. He hurried across Crowther Bridge over the canal and came out on the Briddvale Road.

With a sickening jolt he suddenly realized the cat had stopped struggling. Terrified that Zombie might be dying in his arms, Jack raced up the road.

2
WHO SHOT COLONEL MUSTARD?

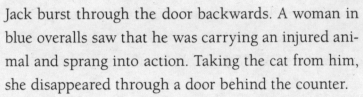

Jack burst through the door backwards. A woman in blue overalls saw that he was carrying an injured animal and sprang into action. Taking the cat from him, she disappeared through a door behind the counter.

Suddenly exhausted by his mad dash through the nature reserve, Jack slumped onto a blue plastic chair in the waiting area. Gingerly, he took off his coat and rolled up his sleeves. His arms were slashed with angry-looking scratches. Examining the raised red marks, Jack imagined his skin becoming purple and tinged with green, as he turned into a zombie.

"You did the right thing" – Jack jumped at the sound of the vet's voice – "bringing the cat to me."

The vet was smiling at him as she picked up the phone on the counter. Jack listened as she told someone – the owner he guessed – that his ginger tomcat, whose real name turned out to be Colonel Mustard, had been brought in. She reassured the owner that the cat had not been run over. Jack noticed she didn't tell them that Colonel Mustard had been shot.

Hanging up the phone, the vet took a first-aid kit from beneath the counter and came to sit beside him, introducing herself as Jess. She set about cleaning the scratches on his arms with antiseptic wipes. It stung and Jack tried hard not to wince.

"Where did you find Colonel Mustard?" she asked.

"In Aves Wood." Jack told her the story of how he'd found and rescued the cat.

"You were very brave to pick him up." She unscrewed a tube of cream. "He's really gone to town on your arms." She started dabbing the cream onto Jack's scratches.

"Will the cat be OK?" Jack swallowed, thinking of the moment the cat had stopped struggling in his arms. "He's not going to die, is he?"

"He's asleep now. Once we've fixed him up, he'll be OK." She smiled reassuringly. "He's lost a lot of blood and that back leg is a mess, but he'll live to eat a few more fish suppers, don't you worry."

"What happened to him? It looked like he'd been shot!"

"Yes." The vet's expression became sombre. "That is what it looks like, although there's no bullet in his leg. It's a bit odd." She sighed wearily. "He isn't the first cat that's been hurt in this way recently."

"There have been other shootings?" Jack sat up straight.

"Colonel Mustard is the third cat targeted in Briddvale this week. Sadly, the first one didn't survive."

"Do the police know?"

"Yes, and I'll tell them about Colonel Mustard too." The vet put the lid back on the tube of antiseptic cream. "There, that should take care of those scratches. Now, I'd like to call one of your grown-ups and let them know you're here. Do you have a number for them?"

Jack was waiting for his mum to collect him when a taxi pulled up outside the vet's. The driver hopped out and helped an elderly gentleman, dressed in a blue shirt and tweed suit, rise from the back seat. He set a walking-frame before him.

"Mr Reginald Frisby?" the vet asked, opening the door.

"At your service." Reginald Frisby lifted an ancient hand of knuckles and wrinkled skin to his liver-spotted forehead. "But, please, call me Reggie." He walked a step at a time, leaning on the frame. "How's the old Colonel bearing up? Is he being a good patient?"

"He's sleeping. Another vet is looking at the X-rays." Jess stepped back from the doorway to give Reggie the space to get through. "My name's Jess." She helped him to a chair. "I'm the vet treating Colonel Mustard, and this is Jack. He found your cat and brought him to me. He saved the Colonel's life."

"Thank you, young man." Reggie took Jack's hand, closing his own around it. "I'm very much indebted to you." His blue eyes were watery. "My daughter gave the Colonel to me when he was nothing more than a ball of ginger fluff. He and I have been together since my wife died." He gave Jack an emotional smile. "I don't know what I'd do if I lost him." He turned to Jess. "What trouble has he got himself into this time?"

"He has a serious injury to his back left leg, but the good news is that none of his major organs are damaged."

"How did he hurt his leg?" Reggie asked. "Did he trap it in something?"

"No. It seems likely he was … shot."

"Someone shot the Colonel!" Reggie was aghast. "What sort of callous hooligan does a thing like that to a poor old cat?"

"I don't know." Jess shook her head. "We're hopeful we can save the leg, though he'll probably limp for the rest of his life."

"Well that makes two of us then," Reggie said.

"Mr Frisby," Jack said. "Colonel Mustard isn't the only pet to be shot. There's a shooter on the loose, targeting cats."

"That's dreadful. In my day, you only shot an animal if you were hungry enough to eat it, and no one ate anyone else's pets." He shook his head. "If I were a younger man, I'd hunt them down…"

"Would you?" The same thought had occurred to Jack.

"I would." Reggie nodded. "Although, I'm not sure I could catch a snail with this thing." He patted his walking frame.

"I could do it," Jack suggested. "I'd make sure that whoever hurt Colonel Mustard is caught and sent to prison."

At this very moment, the Twitchers were in Aves Wood planning what to do over the half-term holiday. Twitch wanted to build a skywatch hide on Passerine Pike, to chart the birds departing on their autumn migrations, but Jack was certain they'd all much rather be solving the mystery of the evil cat killer.

"That's very good of you, Jack" – Reggie patted his knee – "but you've done enough for me and the old Colonel already."

"The police are investigating," Jess chimed in.

"But, I'm one of the Twitchers; the birdwatching detectives. We're the ones who caught that bank robber and found the missing money."

"I read about that in the *Briddvale Record*." Reggie looked impressed.

"That was us." Jack's chest lifted with pride. "We were in all the newspapers. We use our birding skills to solve crimes."

"Well, isn't that something."

"We'll find out who's guilty of shooting the cats quicker than the police can," Jack bragged. "If I interview you about Colonel Mustard's routine, we can work out where and when he was hurt."

"Now?" Reggie looked intrigued.

A familiar red car pulled up and parked outside the vet's. Jack watched his mum pull her handbag from the passenger seat onto her lap. "Um, it'd be better if I had the others with me."

"Well, I don't go out much. You're welcome to pop round my house and ask me questions, anytime." Reggie paused and then asked, "Do you think you could come before the big storm?"

"What storm?"

"Haven't you heard? There's a storm warning for Monday. It's been on the radio."

"But the weather's been nice this week."

"It can turn on a sixpence at this time of year. If it's a really big storm, there'll be flooding, mark my words."

"We could come tomorrow?" Jack said. "In the afternoon?"

"Lovely." Reggie nodded and wrote down his address on the back of a leaflet about looking after dogs.

"You live on the same road as me!" Jack exclaimed. "I live at number eight."

"Jack!" His mother hurried through the door, her shoulder length wavy hair held back from her immaculately made-up face with combs. Her eyes scanned him. "Are you all right?"

"I'm fine, Mum. You didn't need to come."

"Your son is a hero," Reggie told her. "He saved Colonel Mustard's life."

Jack's mum looked blankly back at him, smiling politely.

"Colonel Mustard is a cat, Mum. I saved Mr Frisby's cat."

"Look at your arm, Jack! It's bleeding!" she exclaimed in horror. "Did the beastly cat do that to you?"

"It doesn't hurt," Jack lied, pulling down his sleeves to cover the scratches.

Jess handed Jack's mum a carrier bag. "It's got Jack's jumper in it. I'm afraid it'll need a wash."

Jack's mum made the mistake of opening the bag and recoiled at the smell.

"The cat soiled itself," Jess explained, apologetically.

"Come on." Jack's mum headed for the door, holding the bag at arm's length. "Let's get you home."

"But, I need to go to Aves Wood. I'm meeting the others in the hide." Jack followed his mum as she opened the boot of her car and dropped the plastic bag into it. "It's important."

"And I was supposed to be shopping for a costume to wear to the Halloween Ball next Friday."

"But I *have* to go to the hide," Jack pleaded. "They'll be wondering where I am."

"Send them a message. Tell them you got mauled by a vicious cat." Her eyes flickered to his arm. "I'll need to keep an eye on those scratches; they could become infected."

"But … *Mum!*"

"No ifs, no buts," she replied, marching past him, dropping into the driving seat and turning the key in the ignition to end the conversation. "Get in."

Jack stared out of the car window as they drove past Aves Wood. There was no phone signal in the woods. He couldn't send a message. And he didn't want to. He wanted to see the excitement on his friends' faces when he told them he'd found a crime for them to solve.

3

LADY BARBARA
GOREMORE

Jack rose early and got dressed. Twitch had messaged him last night, asking why he hadn't come to the meeting. Jack had sent a cryptic reply, saying he would explain everything when they met. Nothing was going to stop him from going to the hide this morning. He'd already laid out everything he needed for a day of detecting. On his drum kit were: a fresh notebook and pen, his binoculars, a fully charged phone and his camouflage clothes.

Creeping down to the kitchen, Jack smiled at Winnie, the family dog, who was jerking and snuffling as she snoozed in her basket, dreaming of chasing rabbits. He poured himself a bowl of cereal, spooned it down and placed a note on the kitchen table, telling his parents he'd gone birdwatching in Aves Wood for the day.

After pulling on his boots and coat, Jack slipped out the back door, tramping over the dew-laden grass to the tall gate in the fence at the bottom of his garden. Beyond it was an overgrown footpath that ran along the back of the neighbouring houses. He paused, seeing a small brown bird with a blue-grey head, rust-coloured face and white feathers in its wings. It was perching on the drooping stem of a desiccated thistle.

Slowly and calmly, he slid his hand into his trouser pocket and took out his bird book. "You're a tree sparrow," he whispered, as the bird pecked at the shrivelled thistle head, searching for seeds. Scanning the index, he found the page for tree sparrow and immediately realized he was wrong. Flicking through the pages of the little book, he searched randomly for the bird, but when he looked up, it had gone.

Shoving the field guide back into his pocket, Jack stomped along the path feeling frustrated. He'd been a bird-spotter for two months now and was beginning to worry that he was no good at it. Every bird seemed to be a different shade of brown, and they were so jumpy, and moved so fast, it was impossible to know what you were looking at. Twitch told him to look at size, the shape of a bird's beak and the habitat it was spotted in, and Jack really did try, but he couldn't seem to get the hang of it.

Having moved from a big city to Briddvale only nine months ago, Jack felt he was way behind the others. Twitch, Ozuru, Terry and Tara had lived in the countryside town of Briddvale their entire lives. They knew the names of the plants and the trees like they knew the names of the roads and local landmarks. They didn't need a field guide to identify birds. Even Tippi and Ava, the two members of the Twitchers not from Briddvale, knew lots about nature. They'd learned it from their nan who was an artist and lover of birds.

The thought that he might not be a good birdwatcher made Jack feel sick in his stomach; it was the main interest of his entire friendship circle: birds and solving crime.

At the end of the footpath, he turned away from the cul-de-sac of modern houses, striking out across scrubland, to take the shortcut to the canal and the east gate into Aves Wood. From behind him came the rhythmic thunder of a galloping horse. He spun around to see a woman in a fitted scarlet jacket over a high-necked white blouse, black jodhpurs and riding boots come flying over the hedgerow on the back of a white stallion. She was riding straight towards him.

"Hey!" Jack yelled, waving his arms as she bore down on him, showing no signs of trying to slow her horse. He threw himself sideways, hitting the ground hard and crying out in pain as his scratched arms collided with the earth. He rolled out of harm's way to avoid being trampled.

Already in detective mode, Jack reached into his pocket and whipped out his phone, taking a series of photographs as the woman in red galloped away. Her mouth was set in a determined snarl, twisting her features. She didn't look back, instead screeching *"YAH! YAH!"* as she beat her riding crop against the flank of the sweating stallion, driving it forward.

The rider hunkered down as the horse jumped. It kicked clods of mud into the air as it cleared the hedge at the far end of the field.

Jack sat up, shocked by his close encounter with the horse. Hadn't the rider seen him? She hadn't even tried to slow down. He scrolled through the sequence of photographs he'd taken with his phone. Who was she? He took out his notebook and pen, wrote the date at the top of a clean page, then a short description of the rider and what had happened.

Beyond the east gate cobwebs, suspended between burgundy stalks of curly dock, glittered in the early morning light. All was quiet. The nature reserve, with its weaving pathways and glades of burnished foliage, was a wild place that Jack had come to love. When he'd first met Twitch, his friend had been fiercely protective of Aves Wood, reluctant to share its secrets. Now, Jack understood why. It felt meaningful to be a part of the wildlife world within the woods.

Travelling down the main path to a familiar bend, Jack glanced up, searching the russet canopy above him for the rusty old shopping trolley that marked the secret trail to the Twitchers' hide. The tree had held the trolley in its embrace for so long that its branches wound through it, lifting the trolley higher and higher as it grew. The pair were inseparable now.

Glancing over his shoulder to check no one would see him, Jack waded through a wall of yellowing bracken that swung back behind him like a door. A rabbit trail took him through a tangle of spiky plants that snagged on his clothes, scattering raindrops as they pinged free. He realized there must've been a shower of rain in the night, though it couldn't have been heavy. It hadn't reached the compacted forest floor, which had been baked hard over the summer.

The hide was hidden deep within a thicket of plants that would sting, spike or tear at your flesh if you approached it from the wrong direction. It was a point of pride for all the Twitchers that their den was so well camouflaged, it was impossible for the untrained eye to see. Built around an ancient oak that grew within a circle of coppiced hazel trees, the hide was a stone's throw from the marshy banks of the Aves Wood pond, which, despite its name, was the size of a lake. The hide had three rooms. The entrance was a tepee built from tall branches. The back room was triangular, the size and shape of a two-man tent, and the main room was a square cabin with a window looking out over the water. A ladder climbed up through a hole in the tepee roof to a walkway that encircled the oak's thick trunk. Above the walkway was a pigeon loft – an adapted dog crate strapped into the intersection of the oak's upper branches and protected from the rain by strategically hung, olive green, tarpaulin triangles.

Ozuru's dad had helped them get permission from the Aves Wood Nature Reserve committee to add the cabin (his old garden shed) and walkway to the tree. In exchange, the Twitchers had volunteered to litter-pick and act as rangers, looking after the wood.

Jack made his way round to the entrance of the hide, unhooked a wooden coat hanger from a stubby branch on an adjacent tree and pulled on it, winching the door open.

"Jack! Up here!" Twitch, a short boy with shoulder-length brackish-blond hair and a shy smile, hailed him from the viewing platform. Like Jack, he was dressed in combat trousers and a sandy hoodie. "I'm feeding the pigeons."

Jack clambered up the ladder, joining Twitch on the walkway. Sitting down with his back against the old oak, Jack let his legs dangle over the edge as he looked out over the water.

"So where were you yesterday?" Twitch asked as he withdrew a handful of birdseed from a pocket in his trousers and emptied it into a bowl. "Why all the mystery?" He slid the bowl into the pigeon loft where two pigeons – one goggle-eyed and scruffy, the other a paler and neater bird – immediately began pecking at it.

Twitch had trained his two homing birds, Frazzle and Squeaker, to carry messages between the hide and his home, and Jack envied him his pets. He wanted to get pigeons too, but his mother wasn't keen. She changed the subject every time he asked her about it.

Jack waited until Twitch had shut the loft door and he had his full attention. "Because at long last there *is* a mystery and a really good one."

"What do you mean?"

"Yesterday, I was on my way here when I found an injured cat."

"Where?"

"Near the east gate. It was making an awful noise. I thought it was the beginning of the zombie apocalypse."

Twitch laughed.

"It was hiding in the ferns and get this" – Jack paused for dramatic effect – "it had been shot!"

"Shot!" Twitch's shock was exactly the reaction Jack had been hoping for.

"Yeah. Its back left leg was hanging all wrong and there was blood everywhere."

Twitch dusted off his hands, wiping them on his trousers, as he and sat down beside Jack. "What did you do?"

"I saved its life," Jack said nonchalantly. "I picked it up and carried it all the way to the vet on Briddvale Road."

"Was it unconscious?"

"No."

"Injured cats are vicious." Twitch looked sceptical. "I wouldn't pick one up."

"You wouldn't?" Jack was surprised.

"Didn't it go for you?"

Jack pushed up the sleeves of his coat and showed Twitch the scabs on his scratched arms.

"Whoa! That's nasty. Did it hurt?"

"It did afterwards. I didn't really feel the scratches when I was running to the vet. I was worried about the cat dying." He shook his head. "I wanted to come and tell you and the others about it, but Mum wouldn't let me. She was worried I'd get an infection or tetanus or something." Jack let his sleeves fall back down. "But get this, Colonel Mustard isn't the only cat that's been shot."

"Colonel Mustard?"

"That's the cat's name. He's the *third* cat to be shot around here. The first one died!"

"That's horrible!" Twitch looked out over the pond. "I mean, I don't really like cats, but I wouldn't go around killing them!"

"I know. It's bad."

"You sound … excited?" Twitch narrowed his eyes as he studied Jack.

"Colonel Mustard's owner, Mr Frisby, said that he'd like the Twitchers to look into who might have shot his cat. He read about us in the paper."

"What about the police?"

"The vet said they are investigating, but I reckon they'll be too busy arresting people who commit crimes against people to worry about hurt animals."

"Probably." Twitch nodded.

"Mr Frisby wants us to find out who shot Colonel Mustard, and the other cats, and bring them to justice before they can hurt any more." Jack beamed. "It's our first proper case as detectives." He bounced as he said this.

"Our second, don't you mean?"

"Robber Ryan was our origin story. That case brought us together, but this one we can solve as a group." Lifting his hand to his mouth to make a megaphone, Jack put on an action-movie-trailer voice, "Can the Twitchers solve the impossible case of the evil cat killer?"

"I bet we can." Twitch laughed.

"I can't wait to tell the others. This is going to be the best half-term holiday ever. And it's Halloween next Friday, the best day of the year, and then it's your birthday!"

"Mum's so excited about throwing me a party, it's making me nervous," Twitch admitted. "I've not had a party before."

"You've never had a birthday party?"

Twitch shook his head. "I've done nice things, like seeing a movie with Mum, or going out for dinner."

"Yeah, but this is your thirteenth birthday. You're going to be a teenager. You've got to have a party."

Twitch shrugged and changed the subject. "Yesterday, we went to Passerine Pike and made a start on the skywatch hide. The swifts and swallows may have gone, but we saw starlings arriving from eastern Europe."

Jack suspected he'd be as good at charting migrations as he was at identifying tree sparrows. "Twitch, do you think, that maybe, some people aren't good birdwatchers?"

"You're so impatient, Jack." Twitch gave him an affectionate shove, followed by a reassuring grin. "You've only been looking at birds for a couple of months. It gets easier as they become more familiar. Each season brings different birds. You need to be watching for at least a year to see them all. Wait till you find your spark bird. You'll see things differently then."

"What's a spark bird?"

"It's the bird that makes you a birdwatcher. Every birder has one."

"I don't have one," Jack admitted. "I tried to identify a bird on the way here. I'm pretty sure it was common, but I got it wrong."

"What did it look like?"

"It had a blue-grey head, and a rust-brown face with white feathers in its wings."

"Was its beak the same blue-grey as its head?"

"Yeah."

"It was a chaffinch."

Jack was always impressed by Twitch's knowledge, but it made him feel like they were very different people.

He wasn't sure he'd ever be able to spot birds with the confidence and joy that Twitch did.

"You'll never guess what happened to me on the way here," Jack said, pulling his phone from his pocket. "A woman on a big white horse came galloping across the field and almost ran me over. I had to jump and roll out of her way." He showed Twitch a picture. "She was really whipping the horse. It was horrible."

"That's Lady Barbara Goremore of Mord Hall," Twitch said with a stony voice, and Jack could tell he didn't like her.

"Do you think I should report it to the police?"

Twitch shook his head. "She doesn't think laws apply to her."

"Perhaps she tried to mow me down because she'd heard that I'd accepted the cat killer case and she's worried I might solve it. Do you think she looks like a cat killer?"

"Ha! She wouldn't shoot a cat unless it grew wings and flew," Twitch replied bitterly. "The Goremores hunt grouse. She is a bird murderer."

"You can't hunt grouse without a gun!" Jack declared triumphantly, flipping open his notebook and taking out his pen. "She owns a gun, looks evil, and tried to kill a detective on the case! That officially makes Lady Goremore our first suspect."

4

KINGFISHERS

"Hey look, it's Jack!" Terry called out.

Jack saw his skinny, long-faced friend with dark curls approaching the hide with Ozuru. Terry was dressed in his usual threadbare jeans and royal-blue tracksuit jacket over a faded T-shirt, all hand-me-down clothes from his brothers. Ozuru, who was shorter than his best mate, with a heart-shaped face and neat black hair, was kitted out in a green waterproof coat and trousers. He made a swishing noise with every step.

"Ozuru, what are you wearing?" Jack laughed.

"Dad says there's a big storm coming."

"But it's not going to rain today." Jack pointed up at the cloudless sky. "If there is a storm, it'll be on Monday."

Ozuru shrugged. "Better to be safe than soaking wet."

"Where's Tara?" Twitch asked.

Tara lived near Terry and Ozuru. The three of them usually walked to Aves Wood together.

"She's being weird," Terry replied. "She came with us as far as Crowther Bridge, then got all secretive and said we had to go ahead without her." He shrugged. "She is coming."

Jack felt a twinge of frustration. He was impatient to share his news about the cat killer case with everyone. He'd have to wait for Tara.

He followed Twitch down the ladder as Terry and Ozuru went into the cabin.

Inside, there were eight tree stumps stacked in pairs along the back wall. Terry and Ozuru made a circle with five of them and sat down.

"Hiya," came Tara's soft voice from the door. "Sorry to make you wait. It's just..." She giggled and covered her mouth.

Terry gave them an *"I told you so"* look.

Sweeping back her black hair and tucking it behind her ears, Tara pressed her lips together and looked at the ground, composing herself. "It's just ... I've got some good news."

"Hold on!" Ozuru eagerly took out his notebook. "Shall I do an official meeting agenda, like I did yesterday?"

"What for?" Terry scoffed. "We didn't use it."

"I did." Ozuru looked offended. "If we're going to be an official society, we should do things properly."

"Yes, please, Ozuru," Tara said, sitting down on the tree stump beside him. "I'd like my news to go on your agenda."

"I've got something for the agenda too," Jack said. "Shall I go first?"

"Er…" Ozuru was stunned by Jack's enthusiasm.

"Wait." Tara giggled again. "Let's get Ava and Tippi on the phone. That way they can join our meeting." She made a show of taking her phone out of her pocket and tapping the screen.

Jack glanced at the others. They were all looking confused. Everybody knew there was no mobile signal in Aves Wood.

"Oh! Hi, Ava. Hi, Tippi," Tara called loudly into her phone. "We're having a Twitchers' meeting. Care to join us?"

"Hi!" came a sudden shout as the two girls jumped through the doorway into the hide.

"*Aargh!*" Terry yelled in shock, jerking backwards and falling off his tree stump.

The sudden appearance of Ava, all in black – coat, joggers and trainers – with her little sister, Tippi, an explosion of colour in pink puffer, turquoise top, purple skirt and yellow leggings, got a big reaction.

"What are you doing here?" Twitch cried, leaping up joyfully as Ozuru helped Terry scramble to his feet.

"We're on half-term holiday!" Ava did a dance of celebration. Her hair, which was tied on top of her head in a bun, wobbled with glee.

"The Twitchers are together again!" Tippi sang out, jigging on the spot in her bright green wellie-boots.

Jack was grinning madly. This couldn't be more perfect. The whole gang would be able to work the case of the evil cat killer. Between the seven of them, they were sure to catch the culprit before the police.

"The hide's looking great," Ava declared, looking around and sighing with pleasure at being back.

"I like that sign," Tippi said, pointing at a log that hung beside the door with THE TWITCHERS carved into it.

"I whittled it," Ozuru said proudly.

"Tara, you knew they were coming and didn't tell us?" Twitch scolded her happily.

"Only since yesterday."

"I swore her to secrecy," Ava said. "We wanted it to be a surprise."

Tippi tugged at Jack's sleeve. "I've been learning my signs, like you taught us." She frowned with concentration as she moved her hands, signing the words, *"Have you missed me?"*

"Yes, we all have," Jack signed back.

Tara added two more tree stumps to their circle, and Ava sat down with relish, clapping her hands together. "Ozuru, what's on today's agenda?"

Ozuru picked up his notebook from the floor. "Number one, the skywatch hide."

"Actually" – Jack raised his hand – "I've something way more interesting to tell you."

"Oh, Jack," Tara said reproachfully, "the skywatch hide *is* interesting."

"No, what I meant was—"

"Wait your turn." Ozuru pointed his pen at Jack. "You're number three on the agenda."

Tippi jumped to her feet and yelled as if she were bursting from holding the words in, "There's a bearded vulture coming!"

"Tippi," Ava hissed, "we were meant to tell them together."

"What?" Twitch's head snapped round to look at Ava.

"It's flying this way," Ava whispered excitedly, nodding.

Twitch grabbed her arm. She grabbed his hand. Their eyes were shining, and Jack felt a twinge of jealousy.

"Vultures are cool," Terry said, turning to Jack. "They eat dead stuff. Kinda like zombies."

"Zombies don't eat dead stuff. They *are* dead, well, kind of. They eat the living," Jack replied, testily. Once again, he didn't understand what was going on. He'd never heard of bearded vultures.

"It's a very rare bird," Tippi said, knowingly.

"Can vultures grow beards?" Ozuru sounded puzzled.

"Do you think it shaves?" Terry joked. "Or waxes its moustache?"

Tara laughed, looking happy that they were all together again and she wasn't the only girl in the hide.

"That is cool news," Jack said. "And I've got some news that you're going to—"

"Bearded vultures are not native birds." Twitch spoke over Jack to Ava. "How do you know it's coming?"

"The vulture was spotted a week ago. Nan says it's flying this way."

"It was her idea to sail here, to see it," Tippi said. "She wants to paint it."

"You sailed down on the *Kingfisher*?" Ozuru's eyes lit

up. The *Kingfisher* was Ava and Tippi's grandmother's canal boat, and Ozuru was the only member of the Twitchers who hadn't been inside it.

"What's next on the agenda, Ozuru?" Jack asked, but Ozuru wasn't listening.

"It took us all yesterday and the afternoon before," Tippi replied, nodding. "We're moored by Aves Lock."

"This is big!" Twitch spun round, looking at each of them. "It's *huge*!"

Jack had never seen him so charged with energy.

"This is bigger than huge. It's our opportunity to see a *lifer*!"

Everyone was smiling and Jack's insides crumpled. He wasn't sure what a *lifer* was.

"Jack, you are going to love this bird." Twitch grabbed his shoulders and shook him. "They eat bones!"

"Cool," Jack replied, faking enthusiasm, and trying not to feel hurt that, in his excitement about the vulture, Twitch seemed to have forgotten about the cat killer case. Sometimes, Jack couldn't help feeling that he was somehow less than his friend, because he didn't have a passion as big. He knew he shouldn't be jealous of birds. That was silly. But birds seemed to matter more to Twitch than anything else in the world, and that could sting. Twitch had changed Jack. He'd got him interested in nature. But Jack didn't think he'd had any impact on Twitch at all. Twitch was always Twitch.

"A vulture is a big bird," Tara said. "The best place to see it coming will be our skywatch hide on Passerine Pike."

"Yes," Twitch agreed. "It's the highest point for miles."

"Shall I draw up a watching rota?" Ozuru suggested. "We could do it in pairs."

"Nan's got books about the bearded vulture on the boat," Ava said, "if you want to come and learn more about them."

They were all standing up now. Jack rose too.

Tippi held up her right hand and drew her first two fingers together, tapping them twice against her thumb, making the sign for *bird*. They all made the sign and launched into The Twitchers Oath. They grinned at each other as they recited the words that Jack had helped write, and he tried to smile too.

"I do solemnly swear never to knowingly hurt a bird. I will respect my feathered friends and help them when they are in need.

I will protect every bird, be it rare, endangered or common, and fight to conserve their habitats, or may crows peck out my eyes when I am dead.
For I am a Twitcher, now and for ever."

"To the *Kingfisher*!" Twitch declared, and they all trooped out of the hide after him.

SPLATICUS CATICUS

Jack hung back as the Twitchers marched merrily through the trees to the footpath, heading towards the kissing gate that opened onto the canal. Everyone was chatting excitedly. No one noticed that he was subdued and lagging behind.

A tiny bird landed on a spray of elderberries beside him and chirruped. Jack had no clue what type of bird it was.

"Shove off, brown bird," he growled, and the bird obeyed. He glanced up, feeling a hot flush of guilt, but the others were too far ahead to have heard him. When he reached the junction, he loitered, kicking at a mound of fallen leaves that had collected at the base of the signpost.

Amid the familiar clamour of Aves Wood – the rustling leaves, the churning river and the twittering birds – Jack heard a strange, strangled, hiccupping sound. He lifted his head to call out to the others, but they had disappeared around a bend in the path.

Curious to discover what the noise was, Jack followed a winding track made over years by children going down to the bank of the River Bridd.

Sitting on a rock beside a rope swing was Pamela Hardacre. She had her arms wrapped around her knees and was staring at the river, crying.

Pamela Hardacre was the most popular girl in school and the meanest. Jack couldn't imagine what had brought her to Aves Wood. It was a place she sneered at. And he'd never seen her upset, let alone cry.

"Pamela?" Jack approached warily. "Are you OK?"

"Go away," Pamela shouted, wiping her sleeve across her face before turning to see who it was. "Oh, it's you." She looked past Jack to see if he was alone. Her eyes were red and puffy. "Shouldn't you be hanging out with your feathered freak squad in a muddy hole somewhere?"

"Yes," Jack replied, coming to sit down beside her, "but I heard crying." He paused, waiting for her to tell him why, but she didn't. "Don't see you in Aves Wood often," he tried. This was an understatement. Jack had never seen Pamela in the nature reserve.

Pamela clamped her jaw shut and stared moodily at

the water. Jack studied her, noticing her nails, painted a glittery purple, had been bitten right down. Her hair, which she always wore parted in the middle so that it fell either side of her blue eyes like long golden curtains, was unbrushed and scraped into a ponytail. Something was very wrong. Jack decided he should wait quietly until she was ready to talk. He knew that's what Twitch would do.

"Where are your friends?" Pamela asked eventually.

"Looking for a bird with a beard," Jack replied cheerily.

"Birds don't have beards!" Pamela laughed despite herself.

"This one does. It's very rare. Some kind of vulture."

"Sounds stupid." Pamela glanced at him. "And ugly."

"Twitch says it eats bones."

"Ew! Gross!" Pamela frowned, then gave him an appraising look. "Wait. You're winding me up. Birds don't have beards and eat bones."

"This one does. For real."

"My cat likes to catch birds..." The muscles in Pamela's chin tensed as her lips clamped together in a tiny frown.

Jack sat up, suddenly alert. "Is... Is something wrong with your cat?"

Pamela nodded, looking down so he couldn't see her face. "This morning … in the kitchen … Splatty, my cat…" She made a high-pitched whining noise in the back of her throat as emotion overpowered her speech. "She was on the floor…" Pamela couldn't go on. She buried her head in her knees and sobbed.

Jack sat patiently beside her, saying nothing. He felt sick. He knew what had happened to Splatty.

Pamela's sobs subsided. "Someone shot her, Jack!" she blurted out. "Someone shot Splatty! Who would do a thing like that?"

"That's awful!" Jack said sincerely. "Was she, I mean, is she … alive?"

Pamela nodded as she wiped her tears away. "She was bleeding really bad. We took her to the emergency vet. She's got to stay the night. They gave her anaesthetic so they could stitch her up." Her eyes blazed with anger. "Some scumbag shot her in the tummy."

"Scumbag is right," Jack agreed. "I found a cat in the woods yesterday. It had been shot too. There's someone out there with a gun that really doesn't like cats. The vet said it was the third cat to have been hurt this week."

"Do you think it was the same person who hurt Splaticus Caticus?" Pamela gasped.

"Splaticus Caticus?" Jack lifted an eyebrow.

"That's Splatty's full name." Pamela glared at him, bunching up her fist. "And if you say a word about it, I'll give you a dead arm."

"I didn't say anything." Jack held up his hands. "And I do think it was the same person who targeted both cats. When was your cat shot?"

"Last night, but we didn't find her until this morning." Pamela's anger was helping her overcome her tears. "It's so cruel. Pets are a part of people's families. Who would shoot them?"

"I don't know." Jack shook his head. "Have you told the police?"

"My parents talked to the police." Pamela's shoulders slumped. "They took down the details, and they say they're investigating but that there's not much they can do unless there's a witness to the attack." She sighed. "They didn't even look for clues."

"*What?* Four cats have been shot now and one of them has died! That's murder! This is serious. They should've looked for clues."

"That's what I think." Pamela nodded vigorously. "That's why I came here."

"To Aves Wood?"

"I was looking for your secret club house…"

"Our hide?"

"Hide, club house, whatever," she huffed. "I searched for ages, but I couldn't find it."

"It's camouflaged." Jack paused as the penny dropped. "Wait. You came looking for us? You want the Twitchers to investigate Splatty's shooting?"

"You caught a bank robber, didn't you?"

"Yeah, but, you're always so … rude about us."

"So what? I'm rude about everybody," Pamela replied haughtily. "I want you to find out who hurt my Splaticus so I can shoot *them* and see how they like it."

"You can't shoot people, Pamela."

"Fine, well, get them arrested and sent to prison then." She scowled. "So, are you going to help me or not?"

Jack stared at Pamela. She was exasperating.

"Actually, I've been working the case since yesterday," he said casually.

"You have?"

"Yeah. Mr Reginald Frisby asked us to find the culprit and bring them to justice."

"Who's he?"

"The owner of the cat I saved yesterday."

"You saved the cat?" The sneer melted from Pamela's face.

"Yes." Jack pulled up his sleeves. "It gave me a good scratching when I carried it to the vet's, because it was frightened. The vet said I saved its life."

"Oh, Jack!" Pamela stared at him with sudden unbridled admiration and Jack felt himself blush.

"So you see, I'm already on the trail of the evil cat killer and I intend to get the evidence needed to convict them and send them to prison."

"Really?" Pamela's eyes were wide. "You promise?"

"I promise," Jack said solemnly, getting to his feet. "Now, you live on Greenshank Road, don't you?"

"Yes. Number twenty-seven."

"We'll come over this afternoon, look at the crime scene, take your statement, and hunt for clues."

"Oh!" Pamela drew in a ragged breath and smiled at him. "Thank you."

"We are going to find out who is doing this. And stop them before another cat gets hurt." Jack felt a thrill as the words came out of his mouth. "Go home. Don't touch anything, and don't worry. The Twitchers are on the case."

6
BREAKAWAY DETECTIVE SQUAD

"Where did you go?" Ava called out as Jack made his way back along the track. She had her hands on her hips and Terry was stood beside the signpost.

"We got to the boat and you weren't with us," Terry said, accusingly. "We thought you'd fallen into the canal or something."

"I'm fine." Jack noticed that Twitch hadn't come looking for him.

"Twitch is on the boat with his nose stuck in a book about vultures," Terry said, as if reading Jack's mind. "Turns out the bearded one coming this way is some kind of mythical bird in Iranian culture. Tara got crazy excited. She says it's called the houmous bird, or something."

"Huma bird," Ava corrected him, rolling her eyes.

"Yeah, the Huma bird. That's what I meant. Anyway, she says if you see the Huma bird you'll be happy for the rest of your life, but that if someone kills it they'll die within forty days, which is pretty cool because it basically means the bird dishes out luck or curses," Terry babbled. "I hope we see it. I'd like to be lucky for the rest of my life. Hey, if we do see it, I'm going to play the lottery and win a million pounds!"

"You have to be over eighteen to do the lottery," Jack pointed out.

"Doesn't that path go down to the river? What were you doing down there?" Ava asked as they headed towards the canal.

"Working a case," Jack replied, as if solving mysteries was the most ordinary thing in the world.

"A case?"

"What case?"

Ava and Terry had stopped walking. Jack was gratified to see them wide-eyed with interest.

"I'm investigating the case of the evil cat killer," Jack replied, continuing to walk. They hurried to his side to hear. "Four cats have been shot in a week. One of them died."

"What! That's terrible!" Ava said, aghast.

"How come you're investigating it?" Terry asked.

"Because yesterday, when I didn't show up for the Twitchers' meeting, I was saving one of those cats." Ava narrowed her eyes as if she didn't believe him, and Jack pulled up his sleeves. "Colonel Mustard did this to me as I was carrying him to the vet's."

"Ouch! That must've hurt!" Ava's astonishment and concern made Jack stand a little taller.

"I told his owner about the Twitchers and Mr Frisby asked if we'd work the case. The police can't do much unless a witness sees someone shoot at a cat."

"Why didn't you say something in the meeting?" Terry asked, almost skipping he was so excited. "This is epic!"

"I tried, but I didn't want to steal anyone's thunder." Jack shrugged. "Twitch knows about the case. I told him this morning, but you know him and birds. A rare vulture visiting Briddvale? That's a big deal for him, bigger than solving a case." He felt very noble as he shook his head. "But I won't let Mr Frisby down. I'm happy to work the case on my own, whilst you guys wait for the big bird. In fact, I said I'd interview him later today. I've also promised to visit the house where Splatty, the cat who was found shot this morning, lives: to look for clues."

"Can we come too?" Terry pleaded. "We want to help, don't we, Ava?"

"Yes." Ava grinned. "Let's tell the others and then we can go."

"Wait." Jack stopped. He could see the *Kingfisher* moored to the towpath fifty metres away, its roof covered with a colourful container garden of flowers. "Maybe we shouldn't tell the others just yet."

"Why not?" Terry asked. "They'll be into it. I know they will. This is our first case since the bank robber."

"Yeah, but Twitch is really excited about this vulture." He turned to Ava. "When you told him about it, it was like you'd said Christmas was coming early. Twitch forgot about everything and everyone else, including the case."

"So?" Ava prompted. "He's always like that about birds."

"If Ozuru, Tara and Tippi are excited about the bird" – Jack was uncomfortably aware that he wasn't – "I don't want to spoil things for them. Why don't we three do some preliminary investigating, conduct the interviews, poke about, see if we can find some clues. Then once we've got some suspects and have built a case, we can tell them about it."

"We can look for a giant bird and track down a crazed cat killer at the same time," Terry protested.

"No, Jack's right," Ava said. "Twitch won't be interested in the case with the vulture coming, and I don't think Tara will either. Let Ozuru draw up the rota for the skywatch, and Twitch and Tara do the bird research and plan everything. We'll set up a case file on the cat killer and gather all the facts we can, then we can tell them tomorrow."

"But Ozuru's my best friend. I tell him everything."

"It's only for one day," Ava said.

"There's another reason not to tell the others yet," Jack said. "The person whose cat was found shot this morning is Pamela."

"Pamela Hardacre?" Terry was appalled. "She says we're a dumb bunch of ditch dwellers!"

"Poor Pamela," Ava muttered.

"What do you want to help *her* for?" Terry scowled. Jack knew he didn't like her because Pamela constantly mocked him for wearing second-hand clothes.

"She did help us catch the bank robber," he pointed out.

"To get likes on the Internet," Terry spat.

"C'mon Terry, someone shot her cat," Ava said. "That's awful."

"You don't see her at school, Ava. She's horrible to Tara," Terry said. "Ever since she joined the Twitchers, Pamela pretends she can't hear Tara when she talks. She pretends she hears an annoying buzzing fly and makes everyone laugh at her."

"It's true," Jack said, "and Twitch and Ozuru like Pamela less than you do. But if they knew about Splatty, they'd want to help."

"I don't know." Terry kicked at a stone.

"We'll let them go on being excited about the vulture and making preparations, while we do the investigating," Jack cajoled. "Then they won't have to deal with Pamela."

"Yeah, all right," Terry agreed, as they approached the blue hull of the *Kingfisher*.

Clambering onto the bow of the boat, Ava pushed the cabin door open, calling out, "We found him!"

"Sorry." Jack smiled apologetically as they all looked up at him. "I got distracted by, er, a bird." No one batted an eyelid at this. "Nan, it's nice to see you again."

Ava and Tippi's grandmother's name was Nancy, but everyone called her Nan, including her granddaughters. She was an illustrator. The *Kingfisher* was her home and her studio. Paintbrushes hung in bundles from hooks on the walls. There were pencils stuffed into jam jars on the shelves and half-finished paintings of birds were taped to the wood-panelled walls.

"You're a good boy, Jack." Nan clapped him on the back then pulled him in for a hug. Releasing him, she pointed to the kitchen sideboard. "Help yourself to juice and a biscuit."

Twitch and Tara were poring over a map of Briddvale that was spread over the table in the seating area beyond the kitchen.

"Hey, Jack, come and check this out." Twitch waved him over. "The lammergeier travels using thermals, which means it does most of its flying in the day."

"The what?" Jack hadn't understood anything Twitch had said.

"Lammergeier is the name of the bearded vulture," Tara explained, her eyes shining.

"They roost in high places." Twitch pointed to the map. "We've circled all the high peaks, where it could stop overnight, but I'm thinking – should we also be looking at areas with tall trees?"

"Er, yeah." Jack nodded, glancing at Ava in alarm; she suppressed a smile.

"Once we know the direction the lammergeier's travelling," Twitch said to Tara, "we'll have a better idea of potential roosting spots."

"Tomorrow, we're going to take supplies to the skywatch hide up on Passerine Pike," Ozuru said happily, holding up his notebook. "I'm writing a list."

"Isn't there a big storm coming?" Jack looked pointedly at Ozuru's waterproof trousers.

"Rain won't stop us!" Twitch cried, without lifting his eyes from the map.

Jack, Ava and Terry sat down and drank their juice, listening and nodding at everything the others said.

"You know, I've been thinking about that storm," Jack said, shooting a meaningful look at Ava and Terry. "If it comes tonight, shouldn't one of us go back to the hide and make sure it's secure. You know, put all our stuff into the waterproof boxes and lift them onto the walkway under the tarpaulin." He paused. "I don't mind doing it."

"You'll need a hand with the lifting," Terry said.

"I'll help you," Ava said.

"Me too." Terry nodded, dusting biscuit crumbs from his hands.

The three of them got up, to a chorus of grateful grunts and nods from the others. Tara was lost in her book, Twitch was marking the map, Ozuru was noting things down, and Tippi was drawing a picture of the bearded vulture. They barely noticed Jack, Ava and Terry leave.

7
PRELIMINARY INVESTIGATIONS

"Whoever is doing this must hate cats," Ava said, as they walked along the canal towpath. "I wonder why?"

"Perhaps one of their relatives died," Jack suggested, "and when their body was found, it was surrounded by hundreds of cats eating their skin."

"That's gross!" Terry laughed.

"Well, you've got to be pretty messed up to prowl around at night shooting cats," Jack pointed out.

"We don't know it happens at night-time," Terry said.

"You'd hardly shoot cats in broad daylight," Jack countered. "Someone would see you."

"What if they're not only shooting cats," Ava said, thinking out loud. "The vet only told you about cats, but we should check last week's local paper in case there are stories of other animals getting shot."

"You think the cat killer might be hunting bunnies and gerbils?" Terry snorted.

"Well, you can't shoot at a dog, because their owner walks with them," Ava said. "Maybe it isn't a cat hater, maybe it's a pet hater."

"Someone who's wanted a pet all their life but never been allowed to have one," Terry hypothesized dramatically, as they climbed the steps to the road, "and it's driven them to murder."

"It could be a bird lover," Jack said thoughtfully. "Someone with a pet parrot that was killed by a cat?"

"Something must've triggered the spate of shootings," Ava said, nodding. "If they only started last week, either someone has only just got mad at cats, or they only just got a gun."

Jack wished he'd thought of this. Ava was right, there had to be a reason the shootings had started now. "We should get a map of Briddvale and mark where the cats live and where they were shot."

"Do you think we're looking for an adult or a kid?" Terry asked.

"I don't think a kid would own a gun," Ava replied. "Unless they're using someone else's."

"You know who is comfortable with a gun, and just

got a weekend job on the Mord Estate helping out with the hunts?" Terry stopped walking.

"Who?" Jack asked.

"Vernon Boon."

They looked at each other. Vernon Boon was six-foot tall, heavy set, with a low voice and, despite being in their class at school, often mistaken for a grown-up. His dad ran an abattoir and Vernon's attitude to all animals was unemotional.

"You're right," Jack said, taking out his notebook and adding Vernon Boon to his suspect list.

"Why have you got Lady Goremore on there?" Terry asked, looking over his shoulder.

"Oh, that wasn't serious. She nearly mowed me down on her horse this morning. Twitch told me she hunted grouse, so I made her a suspect in case she also hunts cats."

Terry laughed. "Hunting cats is not her style, unless they were big cats on safari."

As they approached Redshank Road, Jack felt a flutter of anxiety. There was a reason he never went further down the road than his own house; why he preferred to go out the garden gate rather than the front way. It was because across the road and a few doors down from Jack's house lived a notorious bully called Richard Peak.

He and his best friend Tom Madden had picked on Jack when he'd first moved to Briddvale, but they'd left him alone since Twitch had frightened them off in the summer holidays. Nevertheless, Jack did what he could to stay out of their way. Peaky and Madden – as they were known – slunk around the streets of Briddvale wearing tracksuits, trainers and puffer jackets. Peaky was tall, thin and quick to lose his temper. Madden was shorter, stocky and a keen boxer. Together they were terrifying.

"We need to cross over," Jack said furtively, nodding towards a house. "Peaky lives there. The best way to get past without being seen is to use the hedge as cover."

Terry's eyes widened and he hurried across the road with Jack.

"Who's Peaky?" Ava asked, brazenly staring at the house as she strolled casually past it.

"You don't want to know," Terry hissed. "C'mon."

They sprinted away, running all the way to number fifty-two. Jack and Terry took a moment to catch their breath. Ava, who wasn't out of puff, waited for them to recover with an unimpressed look on her face.

The buildings at the end of the cul-de-sac were older than the new houses at the beginning of the street. Mr Frisby's place had a red tiled roof, metal windows and a neat square lawn out front.

They rang the bell and after a few minutes, through the frosted glass in the door, they saw a silhouette approach.

"Good morning, Mr Frisby, it's Jack. Jack Cappleman. The one who saved Colonel Mustard."

"Hold on. I'll reverse and you can come in," came Reggie's wavering voice.

Jack gently pushed the door and they saw Reggie making his way backwards down the hall with the aid of a walking frame.

"Try and keep up!" he called cheerfully, wheezing out a laugh.

When they reached the kitchen, Mr Frisby was lowering himself into a high-backed armchair.

"Thank you for letting us come and talk to you, Mr Frisby," Ava said, as Jack took out his notebook and pen. "My name is Ava, and this is Terry. We're both members of the Twitchers."

"Call me Reggie, everybody does." He smiled.

"How is Colonel Mustard doing?" Jack asked.

"The old Colonel came home this morning, and he's in a terrible grump." Reggie pointed at a basket by the back door where a large ginger cat, with a plastic cone around its neck, was scowling. His back half was shaved and one of his legs was in a plaster cast. "The vet gave me painkillers for him, but he won't take them. He eats around them, and he's furious that I won't let him go outside."

"Poor old Colonel," Terry said.

"If you want tea, you're going to have to make it yourselves," Reggie said. "I'm afraid I'm not much of a host."

"Oh no. We're fine." Ava smiled.

"Good, now, which one of you is the strongest?"

Jack was taken aback by the question. "I guess I am?" He looked apologetically at Terry and Ava.

"Good. If you go into my living room, you'll find an unplugged tele. I want you to carry it up the stairs to the bedroom at the front of the house. Perhaps two of you better go. It is quite heavy. I've cleared a space for it. You'll see when you get up there."

Jack and Terry stood up, looking confused, but they did as they were asked and carried the TV upstairs. When they came back down, they could hear Ava asking Reggie a question.

"Have you any idea who might have shot Colonel Mustard?"

"Not a clue. It's beyond me who would want to do such a heartless thing." Reggie looked up as the boys entered the kitchen. "Ah, good, you're back. Did you see the armchair in there? Pop that into the front bedroom too would you boys?"

Stunned by this second request, but too polite to refuse, Jack and Terry traipsed back into the living room.

"Why's he making us move furniture?" Terry whispered.

"I don't know, but did you see the military uniform hanging up in the back bedroom?" Jack replied. "I'll bet Reggie owns a gun."

"He's hardly going to shoot his own cat!"

"If we're going to be proper detectives," Jack said, "we have to suspect everyone."

"Yeah, but Reggie isn't an assassin with a sniper rifle. When he was in the army, they probably used swords."

Jack chuckled and they returned to the kitchen.

"I don't go out much these days, my hips being what they are, but I knew something wasn't right when the old Colonel didn't come in for his breakfast yesterday morning," Reggie was telling Ava. "He's a greedy moggy and never misses a meal." He smiled up at Jack and pointed to three stuffed grocery bags on the floor. "Take those up and pop them beside the armchair, would you?"

Jack and Terry exchanged an incredulous look, before picking up the bags and carrying them upstairs. This time, when they returned to the kitchen, they both quickly sat down.

"Did you get the footstool?" Reggie asked. "Oh, and there's a couple of books on the small table I'll be wanting. Tell you what. Why don't you take up the table too?"

"Reggie," Jack huffed, "why are we carrying all your furniture upstairs?"

"I told you yesterday. There's a big storm coming," replied the wily old man, his eyes full of mirth at Jack's expression.

"So what?"

"When the storm comes, it's going to *really* rain." Reggie leaned forward. "Briddvale is built in a valley beside a river and a canal. There are rocky hills on all sides. When there's heavy rain" – he lifted his hand and waggled his knobbly fingers as he lowered it – "the whole place floods."

"You think your house is going to be flooded?" Jack suddenly understood.

"I know it will." Reggie nodded. "Most of the land round here belongs to the Mord Estate. They've cleared it, for grouse hunting, and they burn the heather every year, drying out the ground so that it can't absorb heavy rainfall. All the rain that falls in the storm will collect in Briddvale."

"Is that why you wanted us to interview you today?" Jack asked. "To move your furniture upstairs for you?"

"I can't very well carry it up the stairs myself." Reggie patted his legs. "I thought, why not kill two birds with one stone?"

Jack winced. Twitch hated this saying.

"We don't mind, Mr Frisby," Terry said, getting up. "Is there anything else you want us to move?"

The three of them set about moving everything Reggie pointed at, whilst questioning him about Colonel Mustard. Jack paused every so often to scribble something down in his notebook, but the old man had no idea where his cat went at night, or who might have hurt him.

"I did notice something odd," Reggie said, stroking his chin. They stopped what they were doing to listen. "At the vet's, the old Colonel was unconscious, on the table, and the vet showed me his leg."

"Gruesome," Terry muttered.

"She was asking me if I wanted her to save it or remove it."

"Why would you want it removed?" Ava grimaced.

"It's cheaper to take off the leg than try and fix it," Reggie replied.

"What did you notice?" Jack asked.

"Well, in my time, I've seen many wounds. When a person is shot, the bullet burns the skin as it enters. It's hot you see, from being fired out of the gun. It leaves a dark ring around the wound. That's what I expected to see on the old Colonel" – he paused, looking perplexed – "but there was nothing. His hair wasn't even singed."

"What does that mean?" Terry asked, looking at Jack, who was scribbling all of this down.

"I don't know," Jack admitted, "but it feels like a pretty big clue."

TRAIL OF BLOOD

Pamela opened her front door and looked past Jack, Ava and Terry. "Isn't Twitch with you?"

"Nope," Jack replied.

"But he's the one who's good at catching bad guys."

That stung, but Jack tried to ignore it. Pamela specialized in insults that got under your skin. She had a gift for it.

"Twitch is busy with a top-secret project," Terry said, jutting out his chin. "You've got us, or no one."

"It's a bit tragic to pretend that looking for an ugly bearded bird is a top-secret mission," Pamela snorted as she stepped aside to let them in. "But you do do tragic well, Terry. I mean look at what you're wearing."

"Hi, Pamela," Ava said cheerfully, following a seething Terry into the house. "I see you haven't changed."

"Ava, you're back?" Pamela didn't have an insult for Ava. She didn't know her well enough.

"Yeah, for the half-term holidays. We came to see the ugly bearded bird." She paused, changing tone. "Jack told us what happened to your cat." She shook her head sympathetically. "It's awful."

Pamela screwed up her face, attempting to hide her emotions. She didn't want them to see how upset she was, and Jack realized her insults were an attempt at bravado. "Come through to the kitchen," she said. "I'll show you where I found her."

Pamela's kitchen was a temple of fawn marble. In the middle of the floor was an island of units containing a sink. She pointed to the cat flap in the back door. "She was lying there making a weird yowling sound." A haunted look came over Pamela's face and even Terry's expression softened. "I didn't know what to do."

They could all see the traces of blood on the floor. Ava moved to stand beside Pamela, who was blinking back tears, and put an arm round her shoulder.

Jack pulled out his notebook and pen. "Could you describe Splatty for us, please?"

"Splaticus Caticus is a big white fluffy puss cat, with amber eyes, and the cutest little scrunched-up face, and the most beautiful poofy tail."

Jack wrote down: *Splatty (Splaticus Caticus) fat white cat, amber eyes.*

"Can we go into your back garden and look around?" Ava asked softly and Pamela nodded.

Jack opened the door and followed Terry outside.

"Look," Jack whispered to Terry, "there's spots of blood in the grass."

Bending down, they followed the trail of blood to the bottom of the garden and a gap in the fence.

"Splatty must have come through here," Terry said. "She was probably too injured to climb."

"If Splatty stayed on the ground after she was shot, we should be able to follow the trail to the place where it happened," reasoned Jack. "From there, we might even be able to work out where the shooter was firing from."

"We can't go into the neighbour's garden without permission," Terry said. "What if they get cross?"

"What do you think we should do?"

"Knock on the door and see if anyone's in. If no one's there, we can climb over, but if someone is in, we should ask permission."

"Great idea, Terry," Ava said, coming up behind them. "You go knock on all the neighbours' doors, and explain that we're investigating the cat shootings."

"What? Why me?"

"It was your idea," Jack pointed out.

"What are you two going to do?"

"This," Ava said, testing the top of the wooden fence with her hands before taking four big steps backwards. She ran at the fence, jumping to grab the top as she kicked her legs up to one side, vaulting over. "Come on, Jack."

"See you in a bit," Jack said to Terry. "Hope you get permission." He copied Ava's fence-vaulting method, only just making it over.

"What? No! Wait for me." There were a series of thuds as Terry tried and failed to get over the fence. "Pamela, give me a bunk up?"

Jack and Ava exchanged a grin as Terry came tumbling over the fence, landing in a heap on the grass.

"Look, more blood." Ava pointed and they ran, stooping, following the dark trail to another fence. Jack helped Terry over and they scurried through three more gardens in this way.

"It stops here," Jack whispered, hunting around an apple tree. "The blood spots come up to this tree and stop." He peered into the branches, where the last of the season's ripe apples hung, and saw blood. "I think Splatty was up this tree when she was shot."

"Let's see." Ava wrapped her hands around the lowest branch of the apple tree and lifted her legs, hooking them over and spinning herself into a sitting position.

Climbing up behind her, Jack used the joints of branches as footholds.

"Um, I might look around here some more," Terry said. "You know, be the man on the ground." He suppressed a squeal as he trod on a mouldering apple.

"You can see my house from here; well, my roof." Jack pointed.

"There are six houses that have a clear view of this tree. The people whose garden this is, both their neighbours," Ava said, taking a three-hundred-and-sixty-degree survey of the view, "and whoever lives over the fence at the bottom of the garden, and either side of them."

"Unless someone was trespassing," Terry hissed, "like we are now."

"It must've been a spontaneous crime," Jack said, ignoring Terry. "You can never know where a cat's going to be."

"An opportunistic shooting," Ava agreed.

"If we find out who lives in these six houses then we'll have our list of suspects," Jack said.

"It could have been someone visiting," Ava said.

"With a gun?"

"We need to find out where they all were at the time Splatty was shot," Terry said, peering up at Jack and Ava. "But we don't know when that was."

"I'll bet it was dark," Ava said. "A big white cat up a tree would make a visible target in the dark."

Jack heard a shocking *CRACK!* and twisted to see the fir tree in the next-door garden rustling as if shaken by a sudden gust of wind. A family of wood pigeons rocketed up out of its branches, calling in alarm.

"Quick!" Jack cried, moving swiftly, hanging, then dropping to the ground. *"Get out of the tree! Someone's shooting at us!"*

9
FLATCAP

"The shot came from over there," Jack whispered, pointing beyond the fence at the bottom of the garden. The three of them were huddled together at the base of the apple tree.

"I don't think they were aiming at us," Ava said. "They were shooting at the wood pigeons in that fir tree next door."

"I don't like this," Terry wailed quietly. "Let's go back to Pamela's."

"I've got a better idea," Ava whispered with a shake of her head. "Follow me." She dropped onto her stomach and commando-crawled towards the next garden.

Jack followed her and, a moment later, Terry crawled after them.

"This might be our only opportunity to catch a glimpse of the shooter," Ava said, looking back over her shoulder.

"Our opportunity to get shot, you mean," grumbled Terry. "We're not really doing this, are we?"

"I couldn't see any open windows from the apple tree," Ava went on, ignoring Terry. "If we go two gardens along and look over the bottom fence … there" – she pointed at an overgrown garden where bindweed was strangling a wild rose – "we might be able to see where the shot came from."

"Move fast and stay low," Jack said to Terry.

"Wait! Let's talk about this." Terry looked horrified.

Ava got up and took off, running fast, then, as if gravity didn't exist, she sprang up and disappeared over the fence. Jack was impressed.

"I can't do it," Terry said.

"We'll do it together. I'll give you a bunk over. Come on." Jack grabbed Terry's arm and pulled him up. They hurried to the fence. Jack clasped his hands together and Terry stepped into them, grabbing the top of the wooden panel as Jack pushed him up and over. A minute later, Jack landed beside Terry.

"Run!" Terry hissed as he sprinted away across the lawn, past the fir tree.

Jack saw a woman standing on her patio, dressed in a towelling dressing gown and pink slippers, holding a watering can. She looked stunned, but before she could shout at the boys, they were at the next fence. Fear seemed to be all the bunk up Terry needed. He jumped over on his own and a second later so did Jack.

Jack and Terry landed in a tangled heap on top of stinging nettles.

Ava covered her mouth, trying not to laugh as they jumped about cursing. The garden they were in was wild and overgrown. The grass was up to their thighs.

"Where did you learn to jump fences?" Jack asked Ava as they waded through the jungle of wild plants to the bottom of the garden.

"I do parkour. It's like gymnastics and running mixed together."

"You're really good."

Terry found a large empty paint tin in a tumbledown shed and stood on it to peep over the fence. "It could be any of them," he moaned, stepping off so Jack could take a look.

Standing on the paint tin, Jack scanned the dark windows. He had a horrible suspicion that the house to the right was Richard Peak's house.

"Up there," Ava hissed, standing on tiptoe at Jack's elbow. "Look, there's a man at that top window."

Expecting to see Peaky, Jack pulled his binoculars from his trouser pocket and trained them on the glass, but he was surprised to spy the weathered face of a middle-aged man wearing a peaked flat cap. He was barrel-chested with burly shoulders. The man looked angry and raised a fist as he spoke aggressively to someone. "That's not Mr Peak," Jack whispered. "He's a thin, sneery, pasty-faced man." The stranger lifted his other arm and Jack gasped. "He's got a shotgun!" He wobbled on the paint pot and stumbled down. "The man in that window has a gun!"

"Who is he?" Ava whispered.

"Who cares!" Terry squeaked. "Let's get out of here."

"I've never seen him before," Jack replied. "I thought that was the Peaks' house, but I know what they all look like."

"Maybe he's a visitor," Ava said.

"If he arrived by car, it'll be in their drive. We could use his number plate to identify him."

"Yes!" Ava looked through the overgrown jungle towards the house. "Look, there's an alley down the side of the house out to the road. Let's go look." And without waiting for a reply, she sprinted away.

"I wish she wouldn't keep doing that," Terry muttered to Jack as they scrambled after her.

The three of them pelted into the street, haring around the corner, and running up Redshank Road.

"That red hatchback is Peaky's mum's car," Jack wheezed, bending over, propping his hand on his knee while he caught his breath. "But I've never seen that jeep before." He pulled his notebook from his pocket and started to note down the licence plate. "It wasn't here when we went to see Reggie."

"Duck!" Terry yelped, grabbing Jack's and Ava's arms, and dragging them down behind a hedge.

The Peaks' front door was opening. The man with the flat cap strode out of the house, swinging his shotgun idly by his side, as if it were a shopping bag.

"Tuesday," the man grunted. "Six o'clock. Don't be late." He reached the jeep, tossed the gun into the back, and climbed into the driver's seat.

"Follow me," Jack hissed, standing up and walking confidently across the road. "Hey, guys, want to go for a bike ride?"

"Yeah, that'd be fun," Ava replied, understanding what Jack was doing. She followed him up the drive to his house as the jeep's engine growled.

Jack pushed up his garage door. "I've got three bikes. Mine, Dad's and Mum's."

"I'll take this one." Ava grabbed Jack's lime-green mountain bike and threw her leg over the saddle, freewheeling backwards down the driveway.

Jack grabbed his dad's blue bike and gave Terry an apologetic shrug.

"Guys!" Terry wailed as he grabbed the handlebars of the bright pink bike. It had a basket decorated with plastic flowers, but he didn't have time to complain because Ava and Jack were already cycling furiously down the road after the man in the jeep. "Wait for me!"

Ava stopped behind the jeep at a set of traffic lights. "This bike's a dream to ride," she called to Jack. He was struggling with the height of his dad's saddle and decided to ride standing up. "Oh, your bike is lovely, Terry. It really suits you," she teased.

"Pink's my colour," Terry declared, tossing back his curls and grinning.

Jack laughed. "Not sure about the flowery basket."

"Baskets are useful," Terry stated, lifting his chin, "and I like the flowers."

They all laughed and whooped as the traffic lights went green. Jack couldn't keep the smile off his face as they pedalled madly, following the jeep through Briddvale. Tailing a suspect with a gun was thrilling and exactly the sort of thing he'd imagined the Twitchers doing.

The main road through the town was bumper to bumper with Sunday traffic. Jack was surprised by the number of people he saw milling about. The town was more crowded than usual, but he didn't have time to think about why as, once they'd reached the end of the high street, the road forked and the suspect's jeep accelerated.

"We're never going to be able to keep up," Ava gasped as they pedalled furiously, trying to keep the car in sight.

"He could live in another town or be driving for miles," Terry wheezed.

Jack was reluctant to give up, but the distance between them and the jeep was growing. "We've got the licence plate, but we can't do anything with it unless we witness Flatcap committing a crime."

"He's got a gun," Ava said. "That's suspicious."

"He could be a farmer, with a licence," Terry said.

The three of them stopped cycling, and stared at the jeep as it got smaller and smaller in the distance.

"I know," Jack said, suddenly, "let's hide our bikes behind the hedgerow and run to the top of the hill. We'll be able to see which road the jeep takes. That'll tell us which town Flatcap lives in." Without waiting for a response, he wheeled his bike through the ditch beside the road and lifted it over the hedge, squeezing himself through a gap. He jogged up the incline of the fallow field and soon Ava had caught up with him. "Try and keep the car in sight."

"Won't it be too far away to tell it from other cars?"

Jack pulled his binoculars out of his pocket.

"Genius." Ava grinned, grabbing them out of Jack's hand and racing off up the field.

When Jack reached the top of the hill, Ava was sitting on the ground, waiting for him. He collapsed on the grass beside her. They both looked down the hill at Terry, who'd given up trying to run and was hobbling up the hill holding his side.

"What's that big posh house over there?" Ava asked.

"I don't know," Jack replied. "Why?"

"That's where our suspect went," Ava said. "His jeep turned off the road and drove up the long drive to the big house. Then it went round the back, and I couldn't see it."

"That's Mord Hall," Terry wheezed, collapsing beside them. "Belongs to Lord and Lady Goremore. They own everything around here."

"Is Flatcap Lord Goremore?" Jack asked.

Terry shook his head. "Lord Goremore is old, with grey hair, and one of those funny moustaches that curls up at the ends."

"Flatcap must work for him," Ava said.

"They live in London most of the time. They come here in the autumn for the hunting season. They throw a fancy party every Halloween. Celebrities and rich people get invited, and they raise money for charity by selling tickets to well-to-do locals. My mum says it's to try and persuade people that they're caring. There's always paparazzi at the party so it gets big write ups in the newspapers. People go crazy around here, trying to outdo each other with their costumes."

"My mum and dad are going to that party!" Jack exclaimed, realizing it must be the one his mother had been going on about getting a costume for.

"Well, aren't you fancy!" Terry teased.

"You know a lot about these Goremores," Ava said, putting the binoculars to her eyes.

"They're good to gossip about," said Terry. "My parents talk about them all the time. They don't like them. Although my big sister worked at one of their parties once and she made good money."

"So, do we think Flatcap works for them?" Jack asked.

"We can find out easily enough," Terry said. "We can ask Vernon Boon."

"Who is also a suspect." Jack bobbed his head excitedly. "When we interview him, we'll pretend it's all about Flapcap, and find out what he thinks about the cat shootings."

"And whether he's got a gun," Ava agreed, turning the binoculars back on Mord Hall.

"Shouldn't we be getting back soon?" Terry looked at his watch. "We've been gone ages. They'll be wondering where we've got to, and we haven't prepared the hide for the storm yet."

Jack felt a stab of guilt. He'd forgotten about the rest of the gang aboard the *Kingfisher*. "How bad can the rain be?" He looked up. "There are barely any clouds in the sky. It if happens, the storm will probably be a flash of lightning and a light shower. You know how grown-ups worry about weather. They say there are high winds when an empty bin gets blown over."

"We can be back at the boat in twenty minutes on the bikes," Terry said.

Ava whistled and handed the binoculars to Jack. "That is a nice car."

Jack saw a champagne-coloured Bentley roll down the drive to Mord Hall. A man in a chauffeur's uniform opened the rear door and Lady Goremore stepped out. Her hair was pinned up in a swirl of black and silver and crowned with a miniature top hat sprouting a short black net veil that covered her face. She had changed into a tweed suit with leather elbow patches but was still carrying her riding crop under her arm. "It's her," Jack whispered. "It's Lady Goremore."

"Where? Let me see!" Ava grabbed the binoculars. "Whoa! She looks stuck-up." Her head turned as she followed Lady Goremore. "Oh!" Ava recoiled, glancing back at Terry and Jack. "She just kicked one of her dogs!"

Jack took the binoculars, tracking Lady Goremore as she stalked up the stone steps of the intimidating bristling with anger. Every gesture transmitted intolerance, cruelty and coldness. He didn't need to go into Mord Hall to know it would be dark and sinister inside, and he wondered what it was that Flatcap did in there...

10
SKY PATROL

"Where've you been?" Tippi demanded, crossly, when Jack, Ava and Terry boarded the *Kingfisher*. "You went away for hours!"

"Keep your hair on, we're back now," Ava replied.

"We've been practising our sign language, haven't we, Tippi?" Tara said, diffusing the tension. "Twitch thinks, if we get close to the vulture, we should sign so as not to make noise and frighten it away."

"Thanks for looking after her," Ava said over Tippi's head.

"I don't need looking after," Tippi protested. "I'm nearly nine."

Jack signed an apology to Tippi, and she accepted it with a signed reply. Then she pointed at her big sister, made a fist, and circled it in front of her nose. Jack laughed.

"What did she just say?" Ava asked. "I didn't see."

"Tippi said you were a pig."

Ava pretended to be cross and chased her little sister into the back of the boat. Tippi shrieked with laughter as she ran away, oinking and snorting loudly.

"Everything OK here?" Jack asked, sitting beside Twitch at the table.

"Better than OK." Twitch nodded, happily. "Nan showed me this website that twitchers use to log rare bird sightings. You can track the lammergeier's journey from the Pyrenees, over the Channel to England. Unless it veers off course, they are predicting that it will pass through Briddvale in the next couple of days. It's getting closer and it's flying with a flock of ravens." He smiled. "I'm taking that as a good sign."

"Why are ravens a good sign?" Terry asked.

"Twitch's real name is Corvus," Jack said. "Corvus means raven."

"Oh yeah."

"Do you think that's why the high street is so crowded?" Jack said. "Are birdwatchers coming to Briddvale to see the vulture?"

"Any bird lover who can travel will, for a sighting of such a special bird." Twitch frowned. "I thought you went back to the hide to prepare it for the storm? What were you doing on the high street?"

"Oh, er, I did." Jack's stomach lurched at having to come up with a lie. "But after that, my mum phoned and asked me to do an errand in town." As the words came out of his mouth, Jack could feel himself getting hot. They all knew mobile phones didn't work in Aves Wood. "That's why we were gone so long, isn't it, Terry?"

Terry's mouth opened and closed, alarmed at being dragged in, but he nodded his head.

"Oh, right." Twitch accepted Jack's answer without question. Jack felt horrible. "I don't suppose you noticed whether people in town were carrying binoculars or going into the Outdoors Store? I'm worried that – if hundreds of birdwatchers come, they'll all realize that Passerine Pike is the best place to watch for the vulture." He pointed at the map spread over the table, which now had lots of marks, dotted lines and circles in red pen. "I think the lammergeier will come this way, from the east or northeast. It won't pass over Aves Wood." He tapped the map. "Because it's a mountain bird, and Briddvale is in a valley" – he ran his finger north – "it makes sense that the vulture would head for Passerine Pike. It's the tallest hill for miles."

"We'll be able to see it coming from the skywatch hide," Ozuru said, sounding pleased.

"Where exactly is the skywatch hide?" Jack asked.

"You know the hidden cave in between the boulders?" Tara said. "We put up a stone-coloured two-man-tent inside it."

"It's really cool." Ozuru nodded.

"You can't see that it's there unless you are looking at the entrance," Terry said.

"And we're going to camouflage it properly tomorrow," Ozuru added. "My dad's giving us a roll of his special camo netting."

"We don't want to lose our spot to the visiting birders," Twitch said. "This is our patch."

"D'you think many people will try to see the vulture?" Jack asked.

"There've only been one or two sightings of a bearded vulture in this country in the last sixty years. It's a big deal." Twitch nodded. "This may be my only opportunity *ever* to see this bird. And it's a magnificent one. It's one of the largest birds of prey in the world, with a wingspan of up to three metres. Look." He spun his book around, showing Jack. "You see these orange-red feathers on the vulture's chest?" Twitch pointed at a glossy picture of a quirky-looking bird. "They're actually a dirty white, but the lammergeier bathes in oxidized earth and grooms itself to dye its feathers red. Isn't that awesome?"

"They are revered in Iran, where my family is from," Tara said. "Because they fly impossibly high, it is said they never land, and that they are the companions of kings."

"Is that the beard?" Jack pointed at a straggly black goatee sticking out from under the bird's beak. "It's not very big. When you said the vulture had a beard, I was thinking more like Father Christmas."

"That wouldn't be very practical." Twitch laughed.

"And you say it eats bones?"

"Yeah. Lammergeiers have a bad reputation because people mistakenly thought they killed the animals they ate. Actually, they only eat the marrow inside the bones. They find the carcasses of dead animals, pick them up and fly super high, then drop the bodies onto rocks, shattering the bones to get to the food inside."

"OK, that *is* pretty cool," Jack admitted. "How do you say its name again? Lamb-er-what?"

"*Lamb – er – guy – er,*" Twitch sounded it out slowly. "I hope we get to see it together." His blue eyes were shining. "It'll be our first ever lifer."

"You said that before," Jack paused, then asked falteringly, "What exactly is a lifer?"

"It's what you call a bird that you don't have on your spotted list, but that you dream of adding. Some twitchers travel around the world collecting lifers, but this week a lifer is coming to Briddvale and we *have* to see it."

Jack thought of the short list of birds he'd spotted. He hadn't added anything to it for weeks. He had to admit, it would be pretty cool to add a bearded vulture to it. Twitch's excitement was infectious.

Looking down at the map, he noticed Mord Hall. "What if the vulture goes there? It's private land, isn't it?"

"Hopefully it won't. The Mord Estate is heathland, mostly – heather fields for the grouse – although it does stretch up to this side of Passerine Pike." Twitch bit the side of his lip. "We would see it from the skywatch hide, but we wouldn't be able to get close."

"Have you ever been to Mord Hall?"

"I hate that place." Twitch shook his head. "It's a death trap for hen harriers, and they're one of my favourite birds."

"A death trap?" Jack was suddenly attentive.

"Hen harriers hunt grouse. The Mord Estate heathlands are full of grouse bred for humans to hunt. The humans see the hen harriers as pests, stealing their grouse, but birds don't understand this." His nostrils flared with sudden anger. "Even though they're a protected bird, and it's illegal to kill them, no hen harrier that visits the Mord Estate ever makes it out alive."

Jack had never heard Twitch talking as angrily as this. He made a mental note not to mention that his mum and dad were going to the Halloween Ball at Mord Hall on Friday. He exchanged a glance with Terry. They were both thinking about Flatcap with his shotgun.

"Much as it's lovely to see you all," Nan announced, "I must start cooking dinner and there's simply not enough room for us all. Yes, Twitch, you may borrow the vulture book."

"Thanks, Nan," said Twitch, hugging the book to his chest.

Ozuru closed his notebook and folded up the map. "So, the plan for tomorrow is to meet in Passerine Pike car park at nine o'clock?"

"Yes," Twitch replied. "We need to make sure no one takes our spot. I can't wait to show you the skywatch hide, Jack."

"Dad's going to be so excited when I tell him that a lammergeier is coming to Briddvale," Tara said, pulling on her coat.

"I'll finish the sky patrol rota tonight and let everyone know when they're doing their lookout shifts in the morning," Ozuru said happily.

Jack, Ava and Terry exchanged guilty glances. They hadn't mentioned their investigation. There hadn't been a good moment.

They all filed off the *Kingfisher* and onto the towpath, waving to Ava, Tippi and Nan. Jack glanced at the greenery behind which his bikes were hidden and walked away quickly.

"It's only five thirty, and it's getting dark already," Twitch observed, catching up with him.

"The clocks went back today," Ozuru said, zipping up his raincoat. "Last Sunday in October."

"Oh! We never asked Ava and Tippi if they want to come trick-or-treating with us on Friday," Jack said, looking back at the boat.

"Of course they will," Twitch said. "I haven't got a costume yet. Are you still planning to go as a zombie?"

"I always go as a zombie! They are literally the best costume. You can be any kind of human you want to be – a businessman or a cheerleader – but then you make the whole thing spooky and disgusting with dead pale skin, green and purple eye make-up, gunky hair and filthy nails. Last year, I got contact lenses that make your pupils look all milky and bloodshot." Jack was suddenly hit by an idea he knew Twitch would like. "You could dress up as a birdwatcher zombie! You can wear your normal gear and I'll make you look dead. We could even get you a fake plastic bird skeleton. I'm sure I saw one in the newsagent's."

"That's actually a good idea." Twitch laughed. "Well, we go this way." He stepped up onto the lock. "See you tomorrow."

Tara and Ozuru followed Twitch across the canal.

"What about the bikes?" Terry whispered to Jack, stepping onto the lock.

"Don't worry. I'll walk my parents' bikes home now and get mine tomorrow."

"Cool."

"And, Terry, don't you dare tell Ozuru anything."

"I won't," Terry promised.

11

A THREATENING SKY

When Jack woke up the next morning, it was dark outside. He flipped on his light and looked at his watch. It was seven o'clock. He pulled back the curtain to see a sky clogged with swollen slate-grey clouds. Burning behind them was the fiery light of an angry sun. It occurred to Jack that Reggie might have been right about the storm, although he was yet to experience one that lived up to the hype of a weather forecast.

Last night, he'd sat up late working over everything he'd discovered about the cat shootings. He'd drawn a diagram of the houses that backed on to Pamela's house and her neighbours'. He'd marked the apple tree as a crime scene and drawn Splatty's trail of blood in red. He'd recorded the time and target of the shot that was fired at the pigeons in the fir tree. He'd put an X in the window that he thought the shot had been fired from. Was it Peaky's bedroom? He'd dedicated a page to suspects, and so far he had three: Vernon Boon, because he didn't care about animals and knew how to use a gun; Flatcap, because he had a gun and was in Peaky's house when the pigeons were shot at; and Richard Peak, because it was his house the shot had been fired from. He also noted that Reggie and Lady Goremore both had guns, but were unlikely suspects because he couldn't think of a motive for either of them. Jack had written down and drawn a circle around the words he'd heard Flatcap say as he left the Peaks' house: *"Tuesday. Six o'clock. Don't be late."* Who had he been talking to?

Once dressed, Jack took his notebook downstairs. As he ate his cereal, he wrote a list of things he wanted to investigate today:

1) Ask Jess the vet about the other shootings.

2) Find out more about Flatcap. Who is he?

3) Interview Vernon Boon about the shootings.

4) The murder weapon. What kind of gun is it?

5) Motive? Why is someone shooting cats?

It was the motive that puzzled Jack the most. Why were cats suddenly being targeted this week? As he thought about this, his doorbell went.

Ava was standing on the doorstep with his green bike. "Morning," she said cheerfully. "Bike delivery service."

"Thanks." Jack pushed the button to open the garage door and took his bike from her. "You didn't need to bring it back."

"Well, I'm also here because of Terry's message."

"What message?"

"Didn't you see? He thinks he's got a lead."

Jack clapped his hand to his forehead. "I've been so busy thinking about the case, I forgot to check my phone!"

"Terry spoke to Vernon last night," Ava said. "He's bringing him to the *Kingfisher* this morning to talk to us."

"Why the *Kingfisher*?"

"That was my idea. It's private and neutral. We don't want Vernon to know he's a suspect. Terry thought it could be risky to bring him here if Peaky is mixed up in this." She looked along the road at Richard Peak's house. "And we don't want Vernon to know where our hide is." She shrugged. "Boat seemed like the best place. I said it was OK."

"Wait here a sec." Jack sprinted up the stairs to grab his phone and binoculars, and raced back down again.

"Do you remember Vernon?" He hurriedly shoved his feet into his trainers, grabbed his coat, and stuffed his phone into his pocket.

"Yeah." Ava nodded. "He's the big guy that is always up for a fight."

"That's him. Not someone you want to upset. We'll have to handle him carefully." Jack waved her into the house.

There was an October chill in the air. The oppressive clouds had sucked all the warmth out of the morning. Jack and Ava's breath rose in plumes of white mist as they passed through his garden gate onto the footpath. Within fifteen minutes they were hurrying towards the *Kingfisher*.

"I really wish we didn't have to go up Passerine Pike today," Jack grumbled. "I wanted to go to the vet and see if Jess has any more information about the other two cats. And we should visit the fishing and shooting shop in town, to ask if there's a gun that shoots cold bullets."

"Good idea." Ava looked impressed. "Jack, I think it's time we told the others what we're doing?"

"No." Jack's guts clenched at this suggestion. He didn't want Twitch to know that he'd lied to him, or worse, that he wasn't excited about the vulture. "I think they'd be cross about yesterday," he said, following Ava into the cabin.

"Hi, Jack." Tippi was sitting at the table squeezing honey onto her waffle and sliced banana. "I am a bee-eater bird," she announced, picking up the waffle with her fingers and eating it like a sticky sandwich.

"Where's Nan?" Ava asked.

"In the shower," Tippi replied. "Do you want a waffle, Jack?"

"No, thanks." He sat down beside her. "That looks delicious, but I've had breakfast."

"Knock, knock!" Terry called out as he approached the boat. "Anyone home?"

Terry was followed by the hulking Vernon and his mate Clem, a smaller, fair-haired boy with braces. Clem was the star striker of the school football team.

"Hi," Ava greeted them.

"You're the girl from the bank robbery," Vernon said.

"My name's Ava."

"Has there been another robbery?" Clem asked.

"No," Jack replied, "but we are working on another case."

"What case?" Tippi asked, leaning forward, eyes wide.

Jack glanced at Ava.

"Tippi, go to your cabin," Ava said. "This is a private conversation."

"But I want to help," Tippi protested.

"You can't," Ava said firmly. "You're too young."

Tippi huffed so that everyone could see how unhappy she was about this, then took her plate with the remainder of her waffle on it and stomped out of the room.

Ava waved them all to the table. The five of them sat down and Jack took out his notebook.

"Have you heard about the person going around shooting cats?" Jack said in a low voice, in case Tippi was listening. He studied Vernon's face for any sign of a reaction that might incriminate him, but his expression was blank. He was more interested in the boat than what Jack was saying.

"Yeah. They got Pammy's cat Splatty," Clem said. "She's really upset."

"Exactly. We were hoping you might be able to help us with our investigation."

"Is there going to be a fight?" Vernon's face lit up.

"No" – Ava chuckled – "but if there is one, you're the first person we'll call."

"I asked Vernon if he knew who Flatcap was last night," Terry said, his knees bouncing with nervous energy. "Clem, tell them what you told me on the way over."

"I've worked at Mord Hall since the beginning of the summer," Clem said. "I muck out the stables and look after the horses. Weekends mostly, but sometimes after school if they need me."

"I've worked there since August, on the hunts," Vernon grunted. "Money's good."

"Yeah, but I do it because I get to ride the horses." Clem smiled a mouthful of metal. "They're all thoroughbreds."

"Tell them about Nick Skinner," Terry said.

"Who's he?" Jack asked.

"The gamekeeper at Mord Hall," Clem replied. "Nick Skinner is in charge of the heather moors and the grouse. He organizes the hunts."

"That's not all," Terry butted in excitedly. "It turns out, he's also Richard Peak's uncle!"

Jack blinked, taking this in. This connection felt important, but it didn't explain why cats were getting shot. "Can you describe Nick Skinner?" Jack asked Clem.

"He's got small dark eyes with thick eyebrows and, because he walks the land every day, his skin's like leather and his legs are bowed like a gorilla's. He's always dressed in boots, khaki slacks, a wax jacket and a flat cap."

"That's him." Ava nodded. "That's the man we followed from Richard Peak's house."

"What's he like?" Jack asked.

Clem took a moment to think before replying. "You know when you have a bad dream and someone's chasing you, in the dark, and you're so scared that you can't turn around to look and see who it is? You just know that you must keep running?"

Everyone nodded in silence. They'd all had that nightmare.

"Nick Skinner is the person you're scared it might be," Clem said gravely. "He doesn't speak much, only barks orders. He's a crack shot, won awards and stuff for it, and he'll kill anything. When he looks at you, it's like he's thinking about how to hurt you. Everyone is scared of him. There's only one person he's nice to."

"Who's that?" Ava asked, curious.

"Lady Goremore. He follows her around like a spaniel. Anything she says is gospel. If you upset her, Nick Skinner will come for you."

Jack could see that Clem was terrified of the man. He felt a secondary thrill of fear at the thought of investigating such a person. He had to admit, he'd prefer it if Nick Skinner wasn't the culprit shooting cats.

"Vernon, are you a good shot?" Ava asked.

"Junior Clay Shooting Champion." Vernon's chest puffed up proudly. "I've been shooting since I was eight."

"Do you have your own gun?" Jack asked.

Vernon shook his head. "I use Dad's."

Ava, Terry and Jack exchanged glances.

"Ever shot a live animal?" Terry asked.

Vernon looked at Terry with an expression that showed just how stupid he thought this question was. "Course! Dad runs the abattoir. You know that. He thinks if you're going to eat an animal, you gotta be prepared to kill it. Who'd you think taught me to shoot?"

"But you wouldn't ever shoot someone's pet?" Ava said.

"Depends," Vernon pondered the question. "If it had rabies or went savage and stole a baby..."

"Vernon didn't shoot Pammy's cat," Clem said, flatly.

"What?" Vernon looked surprised by the statement. "Pammy's a mate. Course I didn't."

"Would you ever shoot someone else's cat?" Jack asked.

"Not unless they asked me to," Vernon replied matter-of-factly. "Like as a mercy, or if they were dangerous."

"Tell them what you told me about Peaky," Terry prompted him.

"At the beginning of the hunting season, Mr

Skinner hired me as a beater, to walk through the heather swinging a stick and flush out the birds. Peaky and Madden were hired as loaders for the hunting parties."

"What are loaders?" Ava asked.

"They go with the hunters, carry the guns and load them. That way a hunter can grab loaded guns and keep shooting."

"Grouse fly fast," Clem said by way of explanation.

Jack thought of how much this would horrify Twitch and was glad his friend couldn't hear the conversation.

"Loaders are normally marksmen, but Peaky blatantly got the job cause of the family connection. He and Madden were useless with the guns, dropping them and forgetting the safety. Mr Skinner got really mad and fired them both mid hunt. I had to step in and be loader." Vernon nodded proudly.

"He made them muck out the stables." Clem's miserable expression told them what he thought about having to work with Peaky and Madden. "About a week ago. I heard Peaky tell Madden that his uncle had a new job for them, and I haven't seen them since."

"A *week ago* – that's when the shootings started. Do you think it's linked? Could Peaky or Madden be shooting at cats as target practice?" Jack wondered.

"That's barbaric." Ava pulled a face.

"It could be Nick Skinner shooting the cats," Terry said.

"No. If Nick Skinner shoots at something, it dies," Vernon said. "He never misses."

"Then it can't have been him shooting at those pigeons when we were up the apple tree," Ava said.

"But we saw him with the gun," Terry pointed out.

"But we didn't see him shoot, and there was someone else in the room with him. It could've been Peaky," Jack said. "Or Madden. Or both."

"Do you think Peaky was trying to show off to his uncle?" Ava asked.

"If he was, it didn't work." Terry laughed.

"When are you next working at Mord Hall?" Jack asked Clem.

"I've got a shift this afternoon. I'm there all week. There's big preparations for the Halloween Ball on Friday, and a party of hunters arrive today."

"We need to find a way to look around the place," Jack said to Ava and Terry.

"Mrs Mulworthy was saying only yesterday that they don't have enough staff to manage the hunt and the party. You could go and say you heard there's work going," Clem suggested. "If you mind your manners, they'll probably give you a job."

"Terry and I could go." Jack looked at Terry. "We're local and they might remember your sister."

"Really?" Terry squeaked, looking alarmed.

"It's a cover story for scouting out the place," Jack said. "We don't have to take a job. Come on. This is proper detecting we're doing."

Terry didn't look happy, but he nodded.

"Great, we'll go up to Mord Hall this afternoon, after we've been to the vet's and the fishing and shooting shop." Jack got up and shook Vernon's and Clem's hands. "Thanks, guys, you've been really helpful."

"I want you to catch whoever hurt Pammy's cat," Clem said sincerely, as Ava saw them out.

"We will," Jack assured him.

Ava shut the door and turned around. "What about Twitch and the others? We're meant to be meeting them up at Passerine Pike in" – she looked at her watch – "twenty minutes!"

12

BAIT AND SHOT

"We can't go to Passerine Pike," Jack said, hoping Ava and Terry would agree. "We're at a crucial stage in the investigation!"

"And how are you going to break that to Twitch?" Terry asked.

Jack fell silent. He didn't want to let his friend down. But he didn't want to spend half a day climbing Passerine Pike and scanning the horizon for a bird that might not show up. He'd probably get up the hill only for it to rain and have to come back down again. It was a waste of time. A niggling thought reminded him he still needed to go and secure the hide in case it did flood, but he told himself that he'd deal with the hide after he'd been to Mord Hall. The new information Clem and Vernon had given them made Jack feel like they were on the verge of a breakthrough.

"I have to go to Passerine Pike," Ava said. "Tippi's been going on about it since she woke up. She's really excited."

"We need to come up with a good excuse." Jack looked at Terry. "Something that would mean we couldn't climb the hill today."

"Ooh, I know." Terry's face lit up. "You could've sprained your ankle this morning and I've had to help you home. You're so gutted you can't go up Passerine Pike that I've stayed with you. Tomorrow, your swelling could've gone down, and you can limp around a bit. No one will suspect a thing."

"That'll work." Ava looked at Jack. "Shall I'll tell that to the others?"

"Yes." Jack nodded. "Although, it would be better if it was Terry's ankle that got sprained. I didn't show up on Saturday because of my cat scratches; two injuries in one week might seem suspicious."

"Fine by me," Terry said.

"Right, well, I better get moving or we'll be late." Ava called out, "Tippi are you ready? It's time to…" but before she could finish, Tippi pushed the door open. She was fully dressed, wearing wellies and a raincoat, with a rucksack on her back.

"Been ready for ages," she replied, scowling at them.

*　　*　　*

Jack and Terry hurried back to Jack's house to get transport and smart clothes to make a good impression when they went to Mord Hall looking for work. Spots of rain spurred them on. Squinting up at the glowering sky, Jack had never seen clouds look so threatening. He thought of Reggie and Colonel Mustard upstairs with their supplies and wondered if there would be a flood after all. It had seemed like a silly idea yesterday.

They entered Jack's through the back door, chatting excitedly.

"Ah, Jack, there you are." His mum was standing by the kitchen counter, drinking a cup of tea. "I thought you were off with your birdwatchers today."

"Er, I am. You remember Terry, Mum."

"Hello, Mrs Cappleman," Terry said politely.

"We're busy today … doing … lots of birdwatching things."

"Your father and I are off to town to do a bit of emergency shopping. We won't be back till late. You'll have to make your own dinner. There's plenty in the freezer." She took a sip of tea. "We're on the hunt for a pair of spectacular Halloween outfits. I need something high fashion yet spooky for that ball I told you about." She shimmied her shoulders with excitement at the thought of the party. "I don't suppose you've got any good ideas?"

"Go as zombies," Jack replied immediately. "That way you can wear whatever clothes you like. You could be a zombie movie star."

"That's what you always say!" Terry chuckled and Jack grinned.

"You can never have enough zombies."

"I've never known a child to be so obsessed with the undead." His mum sighed. "Although," she considered the idea, "it would mean I could wear a designer dress." She put down her mug. "It's such a prestigious event; I don't want to get it wrong. You've no idea how hard it was to get tickets." She clapped her hands together. "After Friday all of Briddvale will know that the Capplemans can party the night away with the best of them." A car horn tooted. "That's your father, waiting to take us to the station." She grabbed her coat as she rushed to the front door. "Byeeeeee," she cried, as it slammed.

"So, you can party with the best of them, can you?" Terry teased.

"Naff off." Jack laughed, shoving Terry in the direction of the stairs.

Opening the wardrobe in his bedroom, Jack considered his clothes. Terry picked up the drumsticks resting on his snare, sat on the drum stool, and failed to beat out a rhythm.

"If you're going to do that, put the practice pad on. Otherwise, the neighbours complain."

"When we're at Mord Hall, you should tell them your parents are going to their party." Terry spun around on the stool. "It might help us to get hired."

"We don't actually want a job."

"Don't we? It'll be good money," Terry pointed out. "And it would give us an excuse to have a proper snoop around."

"Twitch wouldn't like it."

"Hey, I like your Iron Maiden poster."

"Iron Maiden have the best album artwork. Check this out." He pointed to a poster of a skeletal zombie playing the drums that was pinned to the inside of his wardrobe door.

"Gruesome." Terry nodded, appreciatively.

They packed two clean school shirts into a rucksack, then went down to the kitchen and made sandwiches for lunch. Their route through town meant they'd visit the vet first, then Bait and Shot – the fishing and hunting shop – and finally, Mord Hall.

"Afterwards, if the rain holds off, we could say your ankle was better and go and meet the others up

Passerine Pike," Jack said, feeling uncomfortable about the lie they'd sent Ava off to tell the others.

"That would be suspicious. If you're going to lie, you have to commit to it," Terry said knowledgeably.

"I suppose. We should probably go to the hide and storm proof it, like we said we would yesterday."

"Yeah," Terry agreed.

When they went to the garage, Jack offered Terry his dad's blue bike, but he chose to ride the pink one. "It's the right size for me," Terry said, with a shrug, "and I like pink. I could do without the flowery basket, but we can put the rucksack in it."

They rode into the wind all the way to the vet's. Jack's spirit soared as gusts tugged at his coat and buffeted his face. It was thrilling to be on the trail of the evil cat killer.

Jess, the vet, was busy with an animal and couldn't talk with them. However, she had left an envelope for Jack with the receptionist. Inside was an index card with information about the first two cats that had been shot. The first cat, Floyd, was the one that had died of a head injury. It had been found by the canal. The second cat, Bugsy, had sustained a front leg injury and made it home. Jack frowned.

"Jess says she's not allowed to give out full addresses, so she's just put the names of the roads the cats lived on, but neither of these are near Peaky's house." He showed the card to Terry. "Do you think there's another suspect we haven't found out about yet?"

Terry stared at the road names. "Maybe ... or maybe there are two shooters."

"Two shooters?"

"Tom Madden lives on Partridge Road." Terry gave Jack a meaningful look. "That's between both of these roads."

When they arrived at Bait and Shot, Jack realized he'd never been in a fishing and hunting shop. He felt nervous, intimidated by the enormous glass cabinet of guns behind the counter. Terry seemed unphased and went straight to the fishing section.

"Hello, son. What can I do for you today?" asked the ruddy-cheeked, balding man, dressed in khakis, standing at the counter.

"Um, hello." Jack's mouth was dry. "I was wondering..." He paused, uncertain how to put his question. "My neighbour's cat got shot you see."

"I read something about that. Terrible business."

"Yes, but there was no bullet lodged in the body and no singeing around the ... the ... place where it hit, which you'd expect, on account of bullets being hot if they're fired from a gun." Jack took a breath. "What

I was wondering was, are there special bullets that don't get hot? And what type of gun might shoot them?"

"Doing a spot of detective work are we?" The stout man smiled.

"Yes."

"Well now, let me see, there's lots of types of guns." He leaned back and admired his cabinet. "But they'll all leave a scorch mark."

"Jack!" Terry called out. "What if the weapon wasn't a gun?" He held up a black plastic catapult with an orange elastic.

"That doesn't look like it could kill a cat."

"That couldn't," the man behind the counter agreed. "That's an angler's catapult, used for firing bait into the water, to catch salmon." He reached down and plonked a cardboard box on the counter. "However, one of these hunting slingshots, used with a ten-millimetre lead ball bearing, well, you can kill all sorts of small game with one of these." He lifted out a simple-looking silver V-shaped piece of metal, with a wrist cuff, elastic drawstring and a leather cradle for the shot.

Terry put back the angling catapult and hurried over. The boys looked at the slingshot with wide eyes.

"This is it," Jack whispered excitedly. "I know it. The murder weapon is a hunting slingshot!" He reached out to touch it, but the man behind the counter pulled it away.

"You've got to be eighteen to buy one of these."

"Oh, we don't want to buy it," Terry said. "We don't have any money."

"Go on then." The man laughed. "You've done your investigating. Now, sling your hook, or buy something. I don't mind which."

The boys tumbled out of the shop, elated by their discovery.

"It was a slingshot! That's why Colonel Mustard didn't have a scorch mark or a bullet in his body. When we heard the shot aimed at the wood pigeons, in the fir tree, it was more of a *crack* than a *bang*!" Jack said as they hopped back onto their bikes. He felt like things were coming together. "I'll bet either Peaky or Madden has a slingshot. They've moved up my suspect list to prime position."

"But the man in the shop said you had to be eighteen to buy one."

"You have to be eighteen to buy cigarettes, but it doesn't stop them from smoking," Jack pointed out.

"If we have our prime suspects, and we've worked out the weapon," Terry said, pushing off. "Then we need to find out the motive."

Jack nodded. "I've got a horrible feeling their motive has got something to do with Uncle Nick Skinner and whatever is happening up at Mord Hall. Let's see what we can uncover."

13

THE PREYING DEAD

Halfway up the winding drive to Mord Hall, Jack and Terry dismounted, hiding their bicycles in the long grass beside the road, and put on their smart white shirts.

As they approached the manor house, dark windows in the forbidding façade loomed over them. The intimidating historic seat of the Goremore family was backed by a menacing sky.

Somewhere in there, Jack thought, is Nick Skinner. His heartbeat quickened.

A shot sounded and both boys jumped, grabbing each other's arm.

"Probably people hunting on the heath," Terry said, trying and failing to sound unconcerned.

"Yeah, probably," Jack agreed, releasing Terry and shoving his hands in his pockets. They walked faster. "Let's get our story straight one more time. We heard there was work going. It's half-term. We're looking to earn a few quid..."

"Guns make me nervous," Terry muttered. "I don't like them."

"Me neither," Jack agreed.

They halted before the imposing pillars of the porch.

"What do we do now?" Terry whispered.

"This," Jack said boldly, marching up the stone steps and yanking on the bell pull.

"Wait!" Terry called out in horror as a peal of bells rang inside the house.

After a few minutes, the door was opened by a blank-faced man wearing a black suit. "Yes?" The man cocked his head questioningly at the sight of the two boys.

"We're looking for work," Jack said, pointing to Terry and then to himself. "We heard there were jobs going, helping out with the party. Mr ... ahhh..."

"Jones. I'm the butler of Mord Hall."

"We're hard-workers. We'll do anything: sweeping floors, washing up..." Terry gabbled.

"Carrying things, setting out chairs..." Jack added, not wanting to appear less enthusiastic. "Making signs, hanging up decorations..."

"Polishing things, and ... anything you want us to do really," Terry finished off.

Behind them, a white van rolled up the drive and came to a stop. Two men got out.

"All right," one of them called out to the butler. "Got the display case you ordered. Where d'you want us to put it?"

"Bring it in. It needs to go upstairs," Jones replied over the boys' heads, as the men opened the back of the van.

Hearing hooves on gravel, Jack turned, feeling a flutter of panic. The white stallion that had almost trampled him the previous morning was trotting up the drive. On its back sat Lady Goremore in her scarlet jacket and black jodhpurs. Seeing the van, she yanked on the reins, slowing, then stopping, the horse. She swung her leg over and landed lightly on the ground.

Jack shuffled behind Terry, hoping she wouldn't recognize him.

"How was your ride, m'lady?" Jones pushed the boys aside as he hurried down the steps, taking the horse's reins from Lady Goremore. The white stallion towered over them, its flanks shining with sweat.

"Splendid," she declared, tucking her riding crop under her arm as she walked towards the house, tugging off her leather gloves. "Galileo's ready to show." The horse stepped forward as if to follow her, and Jones yanked at his reins. Lady Goremore spotted Terry and Jack. "Why are there gawping brats on the doorstep, Jones?"

"They're looking for work, m'lady."

"I'm sure we've a chimney or two that needs sweeping." Her lip curled as she swept past them into the house. Pulled by the sheer magnetism of her personality, Jack and Terry followed her, finding themselves in a stone and wood-panelled entrance hall that smelled of furniture polish and mothballs. Lady Goremore was climbing a grand staircase.

"Come back here!" Jones shouted at them, but he couldn't move as he was still holding the reins of Galileo.

"Excuse me. Coming through," one of the delivery drivers said, as the two men carried a box the size of a washing machine up the steps.

Jack grabbed the door, holding it open, and nudged Terry, who moved to one side of the box and gripped the bottom, helping to lift it.

"Ta," the other man said, as they carried the heavy crate into the hall.

"The suit said to take it upstairs," one muttered under his breath to the other.

"I'll go ahead and get the door for you," Jack said, nodding at Terry.

Terry hung on to his side of the crate, helping the two men as they lifted it up the grand staircase.

"Is that my display case?" Lady Goremore appeared in a doorway along the landing. "Bring it in here."

Jack held the double doors open as the two men and Terry carefully shuffled into a room the size of their school gym. Following them inside, Jack stifled a gasp as they gingerly lowered the box to the floor and he saw a row of gold-rimmed glass cases. Inside each case was a magnificent bird of prey; dead, stuffed and positioned as if it were about to make a kill. He moved closer. The descriptive brass plates told him the cases contained peregrine falcon, merlin, osprey, kestrel, goshawk, honey buzzard, red kite, Montagu's harrier, hen harrier – and between the windows at the end of the room was a giant case containing a white-tailed eagle. Jack felt sick.

The delivery men nodded at Lady Goremore and left.

Jack saw that there was an empty pedestal in the middle of the room.

Terry stood frozen beside it, wearing an expression of horror. Jack immediately realized he was wearing a similar expression. He forced himself to smile brightly. "What a wonderful collection of birds you have, m'lady," he said, echoing the butler's title for Lady Goremore.

"It is, isn't it." She raised an eyebrow and gave a haughty smile.

"Better than a museum." Jack nodded. "Where did you get them from? Antique shops?"

"Ha!" Lady Goremore threw her head back at this preposterous suggestion. "Where's the fun in that?"

"Then…" Jack frowned as if he couldn't work out where else the birds could possibly have come from and waited with bated breath, hoping she would fill the silence.

"There is no thrill of the chase, gratification of the hunt, or conquest of nature in an antique shop." She surveyed her collection proudly. "If it flies, it dies. That's the Goremore motto."

"You never bagged all these birds yourself?" Jack marvelled, trying to sound impressed.

"I can't take the credit for all of them," Lady Goremore admitted with pursed lips. "But more than half of the birds in this room are my kills."

"Whoa! You must be a crack shot!" Jack said, feigning admiration.

"What's the new case for?" Terry asked, trying to copy Jack's light tone. "It can't be for a bird, it's really big."

A shadow fell across Lady Goremore's face. "*Get out!*" she snapped, and Jack jumped. "Kitchen's round the back. Don't use my front door again."

"Yes m'lady." Jack bowed, grabbing Terry's arm and pulling him towards the door. "Thank you m'lady."

Stunned by her sudden change in temper, Terry stumbled as the two boys hurried away down the sweeping staircase into the grand hall. Jack caught him and stopped him from falling.

"She's scary," Terry whispered.

"The way she reacted to your question," Jack hissed. "Definitely suspicious!"

There were more cases of stuffed birds in the grand hall. Beautifully constructed dioramas with painted backdrops and sculpted floors, containing a series of stuffed songbirds, arranged to look like they were nesting or perching. Some nests even contained eggs. These cases were different to the ones upstairs: they looked old. The birds inside were tired and a bit tatty. A wall-mounted display of ancient hunting rifles framed the bird cases. Each gun was over a metre in length with a wooden handle and extended barrels.

"I can't believe they show off the weapons they used to kill the birds!" Terry said, disgusted. He looked at Jack. "You smiled at her," he said accusingly.

"Yeah, well you looked like you were going to puke on the carpet and call the police," Jack muttered. "I had to do something."

"That room…"

"Gruesome." Jack nodded. "And I'd put money on it not being legit. Nearly every one of those birds is on the red list. They're endangered species. They're supposed to be protected. These" – he pointed at the songbirds – "look like they're from Victorian times. But those ones upstairs. They looked … new." He shuddered, thinking of the hen harrier. "Twitch must never come here."

Pulling out his notebook, Jack scribbled down the birds of prey he'd seen in the room. Then he wrote: *Large new case and empty pedestal*. A horrible thought had sprouted in his mind as soon as he'd seen it. "Terry, you don't think that empty case is for the bearded vulture, do you?"

A rumbling clap of thunder made both boys jump and grab each other in alarm.

"It's only thunder," Terry said, trying to reassure himself as he let go of Jack.

"Terry, I think this case is bigger than Peaky and Madden targeting cats with a slingshot. Something else is going on. I'm not leaving Mord Hall until we've got jobs."

"Are you the boys come about finding work?" came the sharp voice of a matronly woman who appeared at the far end of the hall.

Terry jumped, opening his mouth to cry out at the sudden sight of her silhouette, but managed to stop himself.

Jack gave the woman his most charming smile. "Yes, ma'am. Lady Goremore told us to go to the kitchen, but Mr Jones had to take Galileo to the stables, and we are not sure of the way."

"Come with me. I'm Mrs Mulworthy, the housekeeper." She looked down her nose at them. "I do the hiring and firing around here, so mind your Ps and Qs."

A flash of lightning lit up the corridor. Jack struggled to keep smiling as his heart quivered. They followed the robust woman down the hallway, her heels clicking on the tiles. Jack paused to peer into a library of wall-to-wall identical looking leather-bound books.

"This way," Mrs Mulworthy barked, curtailing his snooping.

The kitchen was cavernous. A young man in his twenties was sitting in a chair with his feet on the table, reading a newspaper.

"Kenneth!" Mrs Mulworthy snapped. "What have I told you about putting your feet on the table?"

"Sorry, Mum." Kenneth grinned at Jack and Terry. "Who have we here?"

"Another couple of boys to help with the party. Can you find them something to do?"

"I certainly can." Jumping to his feet, the man came around the table to greet them with an enthusiastic handshake. "I'm Ken."

"I'm Jack, this is Terry," Jack said. "Our school friend, Clem, works in the stables and said there was work going."

"We thought we might earn a bit of cash in our half-term holiday," Terry added.

"Well, Clem is right. We've a big party on Friday night, and from Wednesday, when the deliveries start arriving, the whole house will be busy with preparations. I need help on Friday afternoon with the set up, and then all evening, before and during the party, clearing away empty glasses and washing up in the kitchen. Think you can handle that?" Jack and Terry nodded. "Great!" Ken clapped his hands together. "Well then, I'd like to see you outside the kitchen door at eleven a.m. on Friday morning. First two hours will be a trial, to see if you can follow orders and be useful. Get through them and I'll pay you six pounds an hour for your trouble."

"That's brilliant," Jack replied. "Thank you."

They heard another crash of thunder.

"I think we should go," Terry said, glancing out the window nervously. "It's dark out there."

"This is the kitchen door." Ken opened it and gestured for the boys to go out. They trooped through it and turned. "This is where I expect to find you on Friday morning." He looked at each of their faces to be certain they were all in agreement and nodded. "Now you'd better get home before the heavens open."

"Let's get out of here," Terry said, as Ken shut the door.

"Not yet." Jack looked across the yard at the outhouses. "Let's take a quick look around, see what we can find out."

"But if Peaky and Madden hurt those cats with a slingshot, then we're not investigating people with guns any more," Terry pleaded.

"What about that empty pedestal in the room of dead birds?"

"That's got nothing to do with the cats."

"But there *is* a connection between Lady Goremore and Peaky and Madden." Jack only had a hunch to go on, but he was certain it was right. "Nick Skinner is the connection. I don't know what's going on, but I'm almost certain he is involved somehow. We need to find out more about him." Jack didn't wait for a reply but ran across to the nearest barn, which turned out to be stables. Three beautiful horses were in pens full of fresh straw.

"This must be where Clem works," Terry said.

"There's Galileo." Jack pointed.

The shed next door was full of bridles, saddles and other riding paraphernalia. The one beside that was stacked with bales of straw.

"Where do you think a gamekeeper works?" Jack wondered, as they crossed the yard. A warning splatter of rain hit their heads.

"I think he has his own house, next to the heath."

There was a bone-juddering clap of thunder directly above them. Both boys looked up as torrents of water dropped, drenching them to the skin in seconds.

"Quick!" Jack cried, running back to Mord Hall, picking his way across a flower bed to seek shelter underneath the overhanging roof of a bay window. Terry squeezed up close to him as lightning tore the sky apart.

"Our bikes are going to be soaked," Terry moaned.

Jack grabbed Terry, dragging him down into a crouch.

"What is it?" Terry squealed.

"Lady Goremore!"

Peeping round the casement, Jack saw Lady Goremore striding away from the house. Beside her was Nick Skinner. He was holding an enormous black golfing umbrella over her head, to keep her dry. The storm was too loud for Jack to hear what they were saying.

"We need to follow them," he said and, without looking back, he sprinted into the torrential rain.

14

STORM RIDERS

Keeping low, Jack dashed towards the trees that lined the avenue. Running from trunk to trunk, he caught up with Lady Goremore and her gamekeeper, staying behind them so as not to be seen.

"Will we have it before Friday?" Lady Goremore asked Nick Skinner. "The house will be full of people all day. It can't be brought in on Friday."

"It'll arrive tomorrow or the next day, I reckon," Nick Skinner replied, with a voice like gravel. He was barely audible above the rain and Jack had to read his lips.

"What about the storm. Will it delay it?"

"Probably." Nick glanced at the sky. "Storm'll pass, though."

"But will we or won't we have it before Friday?" Lady Goremore's voice was hungry.

"There's no guarantee we'll get it at all."

"I *want* it!" Lady Goremore stopped walking and gave Nick Skinner a sly smile. "I don't employ the finest shot in England for nothing." She took hold of his chin. "Or, are you not him?"

"I am," Nick Skinner replied, and Jack found he was holding his breath. He thought for a moment they were going to kiss, but Lady Goremore pushed Nick Skinner's chin away and carried on walking.

"Can't shoot it." Nick shook his head, catching up with her. He tapped his temple. "Got to be clever about it."

"Well then, be clever."

Jack expected Nick Skinner to simper and flatter Lady Goremore, but his face was placid and unreadable. "I'll do what I can."

"What you *can* do, is kill it!"

They passed through a gate into a walled garden. Jack hurried out from the shelter of the trees, but there was no way he could follow them without being seen. His head was whirling. Though they hadn't said it, he was almost certain they'd been talking about the bearded vulture. His insides churned with alarm. They were plotting murder!

With his clothes sticking to his skin and hair plastered to his face, he ran back to Terry, who was still sheltering against the house.

"Did they see you?" Terry asked.

Jack shook his head.

"Did you discover anything?"

"I'll tell you on the way. Come on, let's get out of here."

The boys pelted down the driveway, picked up their bikes and pedalled like fury downhill, towards town. The road had become a river. It was slippery and treacherous. Thunder boomed and lightning crackled as water came down from the heavens like an icy monsoon.

Jack's thoughts were dark, his heart thundering, his emotions tumultuous.

The storm was so loud, the boys had to shout at each other to be heard. Deep puddles, collected in the dips of the road, drenched them again and again as they sped through.

Terry screamed when a bolt of lightning lit up the sky, pretending he'd been electrocuted, and Jack suddenly couldn't stop laughing. He felt safer the further away they got from Mord Hall. He calmed down as they cycled through town and by the time they reached the canal, he was keen to stop and tell Ava everything they'd discovered.

They dropped their bikes and hammered on the *Kingfisher* cabin door.

Ava opened it and stared. "Stay there," she ordered, getting out a bin bag and laying it down on the floor. "Come in and stand on that." She called over her shoulder, "Tippi, we need a couple of towels." She looked at them. "Don't move or you'll get everything wet."

Tippi ran in. Behind her came Nan with an armful of towels and a couple of blankets.

"Hi," Jack said. "Sorry to drop in on you like this, but we were getting drenched."

"Not a problem." Nan smiled. "Now, strip down to your underwear," she instructed, "or you'll both catch a cold."

Jack and Terry looked at each other in alarm and Ava laughed. "Don't worry. I won't look." She turned her back and covered her eyes.

Both boys hurriedly pulled off their sodden shirts, socks and trousers, and wrapped themselves in the towels Nan was holding out. It was only when he sat down at the table, covered in a blanket, that Jack realized he was shivering, and his fingers looked like white raisins.

"I'll make hot milk," Nan announced, going to the kitchenette and taking a pan from the cupboard.

Ava and Tippi sat down at the table opposite the boys.

"You made it back from Passerine Pike all right?" Jack asked.

"Ozuru's dad saw the storm coming and came to pick us up," Ava said. "We'd only been there an hour when he arrived."

"Will the skywatch hide be all right in this storm?" Terry asked.

"Twitch thinks so. He's pleased because it means the other birdwatchers looking for the lammergeier can't set up camp today."

"Is he worried it might ruin the chances of the vulture coming this way?" Jack asked.

"No. He says it will probably arrive tomorrow or the next day."

Twitch's prediction echoed Nick Skinner's words and Jack shuddered. He glanced at Tippi, not wanting to tell Ava about Mord Hall in front of her little sister.

Ava noticed and said, "Tippi, could you go and get some of Nan's socks for the boys to put on? They're still shivering."

Tippi nodded and slid from the table.

"So?" Ava whispered, as soon as she'd gone. "You found something out, didn't you? I can see it on your faces."

"I think Lady Goremore wants to kill the bearded vulture."

"*What?*" Ava looked shocked.

"We need to tell Twitch and the rest of the gang," Jack said. "We can't handle this alone."

"But, what's it got to do with the cat shootings?"

"I don't know. Maybe nothing," Jack admitted. "It's something we discovered by accident when we went to Mord Hall."

"We got jobs, working at the party," Terry said, through chattering teeth.

"I don't understand." Ava frowned. "What makes you think Lady Goremore wants to kill the bearded vulture? Did you hear her say so?"

"Not exactly," Jack admitted. "But she was having this giant case delivered. We helped the delivery men carry it up to this room. You should've seen it, Ava. It was horrible. It's like a private museum of dead birds of prey."

"'*If it flies, it dies,*' that's what she said," Terry added, looking haunted.

"What about Nick Skinner?" Ava asked. "Did you see him?"

"Yes. We were outside when it started to rain," Jack said. "He came out of the house with Lady Goremore.

I followed them and caught a bit of their conversation. I think they were talking about the vulture."

"What did they say?" Ava asked.

"Have you got paper and a pen? We should write it all down, before I forget it. My notebook is soaking wet."

Ava brought over a pad and a pot of pencils. Jack recounted the conversation as he remembered it and she wrote it down.

There was a long silence as the three of them considered the words.

"She doesn't kill all the birds," Terry said. "Nick Skinner helps her. That's obviously why she says he's the finest shot in England, but I don't understand why he then says that he can't shoot it."

"Because it's illegal to shoot a protected bird," Ava replied.

"What do you think Nick Skinner could have meant when he said they had to *be clever about it*?" Jack asked. The others shook their heads blankly. That was the comment that made Jack feel most uneasy. Everything about Nick Skinner screamed dangerous. Whatever clever plan he'd come up with, it was likely to be a good one.

15

BRIDDSWAMP

The deluge of torrential rain had been drumming relentlessly on the roof tiles when Jack had climbed into his bed. He'd fallen asleep thinking about all the things they'd discovered that day. When he woke up, he became conscious that it was, at last, silent. Blinking his eyes open, he rolled onto his side and sat up. Lifting his bedroom curtains, Jack looked out at a misty fog. The view was so shocking that he bounced onto his knees, pushing the curtain aside.

Down below, there was no road or pavement, but a sea of muddy water. The parked cars looked like they were swimming in chocolate milk.

"Reggie was right!" Jack whispered in awe.

Scrambling out of bed, he hurried onto the landing and was met with a strange sight. His parents were downstairs wearing pyjamas, dressing gowns and wellington boots. They were fishing for objects floating in the pond that had been the ground floor of his home.

Picking up a wooden chair, his dad held it over his head as he sloshed towards the stairs.

"No, not that one," Jack's mum said. "Get the wooden chair in the corner. It's an antique. My mother gave it to us."

Winnie padded along the landing and lay down beside Jack's feet, nuzzling her nose into his ankle. She was as confused as he was.

"Ah good, Jack, you're up," his dad said. "Come and take this chair off me, would you? Stick it in your brother's bedroom."

"What happened?" Jack said, realizing the foolishness of this question as soon as he'd asked it.

"It rained a lot last night," his dad replied, handing him the chair.

"The whole town's flooded." His mother's voice was tearful. "The river burst its banks." She sighed, watching one of Jack's trainers float past her shins. "We've got no electricity. The soft furnishings are ruined…"

His dad put a comforting arm around her shoulders.

David's bedroom was really a spare room. His big brother was away at university, studying law. His stuff was still in boxes from when they'd moved house. There were already a few pieces of hurriedly salvaged furniture from downstairs in it. Jack slid the chair, seat down, on top of another. Peeping into the bathroom on his way past, he saw a mound of sopping wet cushions and rugs in the bath.

A horrible thought popped into his head. What had happened to the hide? He'd never gone back to storm proof it.

Jack got dressed quickly, pulling on two pairs of socks and waterproof trousers over his joggers. He tugged his cagoule from his chest of drawers whilst shoving his feet into wellington boots. His heart was trembling. Was Aves Wood flooded? Was the hide still standing? He'd told the others that he'd put anything that might get wet into the plastic boxes and stored them up on the platform under the tarpaulin ... but he hadn't!

He grabbed his phone to see if he'd had any messages. Nothing. He guessed his friends' houses looked a lot like his. He tossed the phone onto the bed. What should he do? His stomach was a mess of panic. The others were going to be furious with him. What would Twitch think when he found out that Jack had lied to him? What if they wanted Jack to leave the

Twitchers? What if Twitch didn't want to be his friend any more?

Hurrying downstairs, Jack splashed to the front door. He paused to take in the surprising sight of Winnie's brightly coloured dog toys floating about in the paddling pool that was his living room.

"Where do you think you're going?" his mother asked. "There's work to be done here."

"I need to check on … Mr Frisby."

"Who?"

"The nice old man who lives at the bottom of the cul-de-sac. The one whose cat I saved. I'm worried about him. He uses a walking frame. He might need help. Can I go, please?"

"Oh! Yes." His mother looked stunned by Jack's uncharacteristic neighbourly concern. "That's very thoughtful of you, Jack. You can go but be careful. The water is dangerous, and it will have flushed everything out of the sewers." She grimaced and shook her head. "What a mess!"

Jack felt horrible as he dashed out the front door. He wasn't thoughtful, he was deceitful.

He sloshed up the street, angry with himself, but he had to slow down because the water kept threatening to pour into his boots. People were standing outside their houses looking stunned and shocked. Others worked frantically to salvage what they could. As he approached Reggie's house, Jack saw his bedroom window was wide open. The old man was looking out, enjoying the chaos in the street as people tried to start their cars and sweep water out of their houses.

"Hello, Reggie," Jack called out. "Are you and Colonel Mustard all right?"

"I told you it was going to flood, didn't I?" Reggie crowed triumphantly. "Don't you worry about me and the old Colonel. We're having salmon for breakfast. We're both fine, thanks to you and your friends."

"Our downstairs is underwater!"

"You mustn't worry." Reggie nodded as if this was only to be expected. "It'll drain away in a day or two."

"You were right about another thing, Reggie. The weapon that hurt Colonel Mustard wasn't a gun," Jack told him. "We think it was a hunting slingshot."

"Yes!" Reggie looked thoughtful. "That would do it. You can kill a squirrel with one of those things."

"We're still working on who did it, but we've got a couple of suspects."

"Well done, Jack. Good for you."

"I'll come back later, just in case you need anything."

"You're a good lad," Reggie called, waving goodbye as Jack turned and sloshed away.

He felt miserable. He wasn't a good lad. He'd used Reggie as an excuse to check on the hide.

Picking his way down an alleyway that passed between the houses on Redshank Road, Jack waded out onto the footpath that ran parallel to the river, crossing under the railway bridge and meeting the towpath at the east gate. But, at the end of the alley, he had to stop.

All of Briddvale was underwater. The banks of the river were submerged. The footpath was sunk. He tried to inch forward but the water got deeper, reaching the rim of his wellies. He could feel the pull of a strong current and knew that moving forwards when he couldn't see the ground was dangerous. A plastic doll with yellow hair and a pink dress floated past as he stepped back. He didn't fancy a swim in the dirty water after what his mum had said about the sewers. With a sinking feeling, Jack realized he wouldn't be able to get to the hide.

Aves Wood was in the bottom of the valley, beside a pond, surrounded by wetland, between the canal and the River Bridd. Staring out at the sludge-brown sea in front of him, Jack realized there was no chance it wasn't underwater. He wondered if Twitch might be able to reach it from the other side of the nature reserve. His house was on the north side of Briddvale, up a hill. It might not be flooded.

As he stood there wondering what to do, a white plastic chair glided past followed by a conga line of liberated garden furniture. He decided to go home. But as he turned around, he heard a muffled shout.

"Jack! Hey! Jack!"

In the distance, he saw an inflatable dinghy. He took his binoculars from his coat pocket. Ozuru was sitting in it, dressed in his fishing waders, yellow rain mac and hat. He was clutching an oar and waving it at Jack.

"Ozuru!" Jack waved back, grinning as his friend rowed towards him.

"Climb in," Ozuru said, as he bumped the prow of the little boat against Jack's knees.

Jack lifted a boot.

"No! Not like that!" Ozuru cried out in alarm. "You'll tip us over. Turn around and sit your bum into the boat. That's it. Now lift your legs in."

"This is brilliant." Jack found himself sitting in the dinghy facing Ozuru. "Where did you get the boat from?"

"It's Dad's. He keeps it in the garage. I was going to check on the hide, but the current from the river pushed me this way."

"I was going to check on the hide too. Is your house flooded?"

"Badly." Ozuru nodded. "Here, take this other oar and come sit beside me. We'll get there quicker with two of us rowing."

"Got it," Jack said, as he slid the oar into the rowlock. "Have you spoken to Twitch today?"

"No, I…" Jack patted his pockets, then clapped his hand to his forehead. "I've left my phone on my bed."

"I dropped mine in the water, getting into the boat." Ozuru sighed as he held up a dead phone. "Hey, how's your ankle?"

"Fine. Why?" Jack was thrown by this question, then his heart lurched. "Oh! I see. No, it was Terry's ankle that got hurt, but it was better by the end of the day."

"Oh, I thought Ava said it was yours."

The boys rowed the dinghy under the railway bridge, struggling as the river pushed them away from the nature reserve. The pair of them paddled frantically against the current, finally reaching a calm patch of water beyond the bridge. Jack could see how Ozuru had struggled to control the dinghy on his own.

He looked about, disorientated by his surroundings. All the paths he knew were gone, entire bushes were underwater, tall trees appeared short, and the dinghy kept turning around. His shoulders were beginning to ache from paddling, and he was about to suggest they give up and go home when he spied the top half of the east gate into Aves Wood.

"Look! The east gate! But wait…" Jack looked around, completely confused now. "Where's the canal? The whole place is like a massive swamp!"

"Is that the top of Aves Lock?" Ozuru pointed. "I think this *is* the canal. We're over it."

"But where's the *Kingfisher*?" Jack took out his binoculars and looked upriver and downstream, but he saw no boats.

Ozuru looked scared. "You don't think they were swept away by the storm?"

16
SUBMERGED

"Nan must have been in storms before," Jack said, more to reassure himself than Ozuru. "She will've known what to do."

"Do you think we should still try and get to the hide?" Ozuru looked anxious.

Jack wasn't sure any more, but he desperately needed to know how badly damaged the hide was. "I think we should try."

Opening the east gate from an inflatable dinghy on moving water was a complex and wobbly manoeuvre, but they managed it without falling out of the boat. Jack and Ozuru rowed down the avenue of trees, floating above the path. The nature reserve looked like a fairy-tale swamp. A spectral mist drifted lazily between the trees whilst mallards swam about acting like the emerald-headed kings of this new land.

"The shopping trolley!" Jack cried out, delighted to see something familiar in this disconcertingly watery world. "Do you think the trolley got stuck in the tree in a previous flood, years and years ago? I'll bet it did."

"Jack, we won't be able to row the boat through the trees to the hide, they're too close together." Ozuru peered over the side of the dinghy. "How deep do you think the water is here?"

"A metre," Jack guessed. "Maybe less."

Ozuru swung his legs out over the side and carefully lowered himself until he was standing in the water. It came up to his thighs. Making his way to the front of the boat, he took the rope and waded forward, pulling the dingy. Jack wished he owned a pair of fisherman's trousers. They would be very handy right now.

Ozuru had to take a roundabout route to get the boat through the trees. "Everything looks so different," he said nervously. "I'm scared of sinking into a bog."

"Maybe we should turn back," Jack said, getting more worried with every step his friend took. "This is too dangerous."

"Wow!" Ozuru halted. Jack followed his gaze beyond the edge of the trees, and saw the huge lake that had not been there yesterday.

"The river must've flooded into the pond when it burst its banks," Jack said, awed by the great expanse of shimmering water. "Do you think the hide is along the water's edge?"

"It could be in the lake," Ozuru said, turning around. "Help me get back in. We'll row there."

As they steered the dinghy over submerged reeds, Jack felt like he was in a dream. The swamp world was so quiet. There was no sound of traffic. No human voices. Only dripping, splashing, pouring, slurping – and birdsong. This morning the birds seemed to be singing as if their lives depended on it.

Jack scanned the trees sticking out of the water, searching for the viewing platform above the hide. He spotted colour and movement, then a glimpse of white skin and blond hair.

"Twitch!" he yelled, making Ozuru jump.

Twitch spotted them and waved.

Jack picked up the oar and began rowing madly. When they reached the copse of trees that encircled the hide, he grabbed one of the coppiced hazels and pulled the dinghy towards it so Ozuru could tie the boat up. The hide door was gone, and *THE TWITCHERS* sign was dangling from a high branch of the oak tree.

Twitch's grinning head poked over the viewing platform. A moment later the end of a rope came dangling down. Jack grabbed onto it and climbed up. Ozuru shook his head, slid into the water, waded to the ladder still strapped to the oak tree and climbed that instead.

"Isn't the world strange today?" Twitch said, looking pleased about it, as Jack and Ozuru sat down on the platform beside him. He was wearing a large pair of waders that he'd had to tie around his chest because they were too big for him. Underneath, he had on a wetsuit. "Nature is a powerful thing."

"What are you doing?" Ozuru asked, pointing at a bundle of sticks.

"Making rafts for floating nests," Twitch replied. "I found a great crested grebe nest, with eggs, floating on the water. It was getting pulled apart by the current. I didn't want to touch it, because hopefully the birds will return to it, so I made a raft of twigs and slipped it under the nest to make it more buoyant. I thought I should make a few more, just in case."

The three of them looked about, swinging their legs above the water as they took in the damage. Jack felt wretched as he noticed that their gear in the cabin had been washed away and there was no sign of the plastic crate.

"I didn't think anyone else would be able to get here," Twitch said.

"I wouldn't have been able to come if Ozuru hadn't showed up with his boat," Jack said. "The flooding is serious down my way."

"My road isn't flooded, because it's on a hill, but it's like a waterfall. We had to bring the chickens and the pigeons into the house last night, the weather was that bad."

"Where did you put them?"

"The hens went into the living room and immediately got comfy on the sofa. I moved the pigeons' nest boxes into my bedroom."

"I'll bet Dodo was happy," Jack said. "She hates the rain."

"And she loves the living room. I don't think we're ever going to get her out of there. Eggbum laid an egg in front of the TV this morning!" Twitch laughed.

"The hide is ruined," Ozuru said mournfully, looking down at the water swirling around beneath them.

"The door's been torn off and swept up into that tree," Jack said, surveying the wreckage.

"How could a door get swept into a tree?" Twitch chuckled. "There wasn't a tsunami."

"Well, how did it get there then?"

"I took it off and put it there," Twitch said. "I pulled out the weaker branches from the tepee and back room too. I made channels for the water to flow through. I thought it might help stop the hide from being completely swept away and it seems to have worked. The damage isn't too bad. We'll be able to fix it, after the water drains away. There'll be mud and silt everywhere, but we'll be able to use it to make the foundations even stronger."

Jack looked at his friend with amazement. Twitch never expected things to be easy, and he never grumbled when things were hard work. He just got on with it and found pleasure in doing so. "When did you do all that?"

"After Ozuru's dad dropped me home from Passerine Pike, I changed into my wet gear and came here. If you've lived in Briddvale all your life, you know it's going to flood when the rain's that heavy." He looked at Jack with a puzzled expression. "When I got here, all our stuff was still down in the cabin. I thought you'd packed it into the plastic boxes?"

Jack felt his neck going red. His mouth opened but he couldn't think of what to say. He didn't want to tell more lies, but how could he tell Twitch the truth without his friend judging him? The horrible silence seemed to go on for ever. Seeing Jack's discomfort,

Twitch said, "Not to worry. I sorted it. I wasn't sure how high the water was going to rise so I carried all our birdwatching kit to the *Kingfisher*."

"You went to the *Kingfisher*?" Jack's heart was jerking about erratically and his voice was high. This was it. He was about to be found out. Twitch knew about the lies. He must be testing him.

"I missed you and Terry by minutes. I'm glad your ankle's better by the way."

"Terry's ankle," Jack corrected him weakly, unable to meet Twitch's eyes. "It was just bruised." He felt like the lowest of the low. He was a slug. No one liked slugs.

"Tippi told me you and Terry got soaked and went home wearing Nan's clothes." Twitch laughed.

Jack nodded miserably as he lied again. "Terry's ankle got better. We'd been planning to cycle up to Passerine Pike car park and meet you guys, but the storm beat us back."

"The *Kingfisher*'s gone," Ozuru said. "We thought they might've been shipwrecked or washed out to sea."

"Not Nan," Twitch said. "She was worried about her mooring, thought the river was going to burst its banks and, because of the junction where the river meets the canal, she said there was a risk of capsizing if the water level rose above the embankment in the night."

155

"What did she do?" Jack asked, relieved they were talking about something else.

"They drove the *Kingfisher* up the canal to the Rosefinch Marina, for a safer mooring."

"Good job she did," Jack said. "The towpath is completely submerged."

"The whole of the high street is underwater," Twitch nodded. "I saw Mr Bettany outside the newsagent's this morning. All his stock is ruined."

The three of them stared out over the lake.

"What do we do now?" Jack said.

"Wait for the water to subside," Twitch replied.

"What about the lammergeier?" Ozuru asked.

For a second Jack didn't know what Ozuru was talking about. Then he remembered that lammergeier was the fancy name for the bearded vulture.

"It'll come," Twitch said, happily. "The weather forecast is clear for the next week. I think the vulture will enter Briddvale skies tomorrow or the next day."

And all of Lady Goremore's gruesome plans for Twitch's prized lifer came back to Jack in an instant.

17

ROSEFINCH MARINA

"Twitch…" Jack couldn't think of a good way to explain everything that had been going on. He knew Lady Goremore's collection of dead birds would really upset his friend, but Twitch needed to know about the threat to the vulture. He felt nauseous. Whatever he said, Twitch was going to be cross. "I need to talk to you about something."

"Is it about trick-or-treating on Friday?" Twitch asked. "Because I liked your idea of dressing up as a zombie birdwatcher. Shall I come over to yours in the afternoon? You've got all the zombie make-up. Hey, maybe we should all dress up as zombie birdwatchers, and be the zombie Twitchers." He grinned. "That'd be cool!"

Jack's brain stalled. He'd been so caught up in the investigation that he'd totally forgotten about going trick-or-treating. Friday was Halloween *and* the day of the party at Mord Hall. He couldn't do both! He cursed himself inwardly. Here was yet another thing he'd messed up. "Um, yeah, about that…"

"Don't tell me, you were planning to go as a vampire." Twitch laughed.

"No. It's… It's just…" Jack heard himself stuttering. His heart felt like it was trying to burst out of his chest. All the things he wanted to say fled from his head. "Twitch, I'm worried someone might be planning to kill the bearded vulture…"

"Kill it? Ha! Don't be ridiculous." Twitch shook his head disbelievingly. "First of all, that would be a serious crime. Secondly, every bird-lover in the country is following its flight. No one would ever get away with it. They'd be caught, and thirdly, no one is that, well … *evil*. The lammergeier is an endangered species."

Jack could see he was about to get another lecture on the amazingness of the bearded vulture, and, a bit taken aback by Twitch's dismissal, he persisted. "But some people think they're above the law. What if…"

"Oh!" Twitch narrowed his eyes and smiled. "I know what's going on here."

"You do?" Jack's heart nearly stopped.

"You're playing at being a detective again, aren't you?" Twitch laughed. "Like you did with the evil cat killer."

"What evil cat killer?" Ozuru looked confused.

"When he rescued that cat, Jack concocted a case to solve over half-term. The case of the evil cat killer!"

"There's a cat killer on the loose?" Ozuru looked at Jack.

"Not really. He made it up," Twitch said. "But that was before Ava and Tippi came, and we learned about the lammergeier."

"I didn't make it up!" Jack protested.

Twitch leaned towards Ozuru. "His primary suspect was Lady Goremore!"

Twitch and Ozuru burst out laughing.

Jack looked at them, speechless. He hadn't made up the case of the evil cat killer. He'd been working hard to solve it. He wasn't *playing* at being a detective! He was hurt by Twitch's laughter. He'd tried so hard to learn about birds and love the things that Twitch did, but Twitch thought Jack's desire to be a detective was stupid! His blood began to boil. He was a good detective. He'd worked out what the weapon was that had hurt the cats. He'd narrowed down the suspects. He'd gone undercover at Mord Hall, and his sleuthing had revealed that Twitch's precious bearded bird was the target of a murder plot!

"There's more to life than birds…" Jack snapped, a squall of anger, hurt and frustration swirling inside him.

"Twitch! Ozuru! Jack!" Tara called out. She was paddling towards them in a red kayak, wearing a yellow life jacket and helmet. "Is the hide OK?"

"It will be," Twitch replied, with a friendly wave.

"Twitch did a great job of making sure it didn't get washed away," Ozuru said.

Jack's anger flared again. Why did Twitch always have to be such an angel?

"Jack," Tara called up, "did you put the binoculars and the books into the plastic box?" Her brow was furrowed. "I've been worrying all night. The books are from the library and my dad's guide to wildflowers was among them."

Jack felt a fresh pang of guilt. He hadn't.

"They're safe," Twitch said. "I took them to the *Kingfisher.*"

"You're a hero." Tara beamed warmly at him.

"Isn't he just," Jack said, unable to keep the bitterness from his voice.

Twitch glanced at him, but Jack avoided his eyes. "If everything's all right here" – he got up – "I'd better go. Mum said I have to help clean up our house. It's a wreck."

"I came here to *avoid* cleaning up," said Ozuru, looking pleased with himself.

"How will you get back?" Twitch asked.

"I'll wade." Jack leaned back, yanking off his boots and peeling off his socks. Balling them up, he put a pair in each pocket. Getting to his feet, he pulled up his joggers and waterproof trousers as high as they would go, till the elasticated cuffs started cutting off the blood circulation in his thighs. "See?"

"You could cut your foot," Ozuru said.

"I'll put the boots back on. This way it doesn't matter if they fill with water."

"Oh, OK." Ozuru, Twitch and Tara watched Jack with amused disbelief as he pulled his boots on.

Jack fumed as he felt their eyes watching him climb down the ladder. He tried not to wince as his boots filled with freezing cold water.

He'd show Twitch who was the real detective.

"Ozuru, you should give him a lift," Twitch said.

"I don't want one!" Jack shouted.

"Are you OK?" Tara asked softly as he waded past her kayak.

"I'm fine." He gave her a forced smile.

Concentrating on putting one foot in front of the other, Jack headed towards the trees, hoping to find a way back to the footpath. He tried to look confident and sure-footed, as he slipped and skidded on the uneven, unseeable undergrowth, aware that they were watching him.

They're probably hoping I fall, Jack thought angrily. Give them another good laugh.

He wanted to find Ava and Terry. They knew he wasn't playing at being a detective. They took him seriously. They understood him, and he wanted to talk to them about the case.

Jack's spirits rose when he spotted the shopping trolley. He felt the compacted earth of the footpath under his feet. The water was only knee-deep here and it was relatively easy to wade to the towpath.

One thing Twitch had said stuck in Jack's head: every bird-lover was following the vulture's journey, so if someone tried to kill it, they'd be caught. Jack had a vision of Nick Skinner's wily face as he tapped his temple and said, *"Can't shoot it. Got to be clever about it."* How, exactly, was Nick Skinner being clever? That's what Jack wanted to find out.

It took an hour of careful wading up the drowned towpath for Jack to reach the Rosefinch Marina. He was freezing cold and shivering by the time he arrived. The marina was bursting with boats that had had the same idea as Nan. He found the *Kingfisher* nestling among them and knocked on the door.

"It's Jack," Tippi proclaimed with delight.

"Boots off. Leave them outside." Nan handed him a small towel. "Dry your feet."

Tippi laughed when she saw Jack's feet were bare. "Where are your socks?"

Jack moved his hands as if he were doing a magic trick, then pulled them out of his pockets. "Ta-dah!"

"Nice of you to come find us." Ava smiled at him from the table.

"Are you hungry, Jack?" Nan asked. "We were about to have lunch. Cheese and tomato sandwiches. Want to join us?"

"Yes, please." Jack was starving. He hadn't eaten any breakfast. He sat down opposite Ava.

What is it? Ava mouthed, able to see that something was wrong.

"I thought of something," Jack whispered.

"What are you whispering about?" Tippi said, carrying a plate of sandwiches over to the table.

"Nothing." Jack smiled at her. "These sandwiches look delicious."

"They're just sandwiches." Tippi narrowed her eyes, scrutinizing Jack's face. "Is it a secret?" She looked at Ava. "It is, isn't it? Tell me. Please."

"There is no secret." Jack picked up a sandwich.

Tippi frowned, eyeing Jack suspiciously. "I don't believe you."

"Urgh! Go away, Tippi." Ava shooed her. "You shouldn't earwig other people's conversations."

"You just want me to go away so you can be in private." She puckered up her lips and made kissing noises.

Ava grabbed the cushion beside her and hurled it at her little sister. It was right on target, smacking Tippi in the face.

Tippi's lip quivered, and she ran out of the room, bursting into tears. Nan shot Ava an unimpressed look and went after her.

"Ava, what day is it today?" Jack asked.

"Tuesday."

"Right. Do you remember what Nick Skinner said when he left Peaky's house?"

Ava's brown eyes grew wide. "He said … *'Tuesday, six o'clock, don't be late.'*"

Jack nodded. "What if the cat shootings and the plot to kill the vulture are connected?"

"You think the meeting is about the vulture?"

"It could be. I keep thinking about what Nick Skinner said, about being clever. He's obviously got a plan…"

"But we don't know where the meeting's happening."

"But we do know it's happening today and who's going to it," Jack pointed out. "All we have to do is follow one of them."

Under the table, Jack saw the plastic box of stuff that Twitch had brought from the hide. In it was a pile of books. The top one was called *A Pocket Guide to Birds of Prey*. A bookmark was poking out of it. Removing the lid, he lifted the book out, opening it at the section about vultures. "We might need this."

"You said that we should tell Twitch and the others," Ava reminded him.

"Yeah, well, I just tried." Jack sighed dejectedly. "Twitch laughed at me and said I was making things up so I could play at being a detective."

"He didn't!" Ava was shocked.

"He did." Ava's outrage made Jack feel better about being angry with Twitch. "We'll see what he thinks of our detective skills when we save the bearded vulture *and* catch the evil cat killer without him." He took a bite of his sandwich and looked out of the window as he chewed. "How long do you think it'll take for the water to go down?"

"Nan said there are ways of moving water down the canal, and that the bulk of the water will go quite quickly, but that it could take a couple of weeks before the water levels are back to normal."

"A couple of weeks!"

"And that's only if it doesn't rain again."

"I'd better get myself a pair of waders." Jack took a swig of squash. "We need to find Terry if we're going to spy on the meeting at six o'clock."

The door opened and Nan came in. Tippi was hugging her and hiding behind her thigh. "Tippi is upset that you threw the cushion at her."

Ava rolled her eyes. "She was making gross noises and saying I wanted to kiss Jack."

"I was only joking," Tippi mumbled into Nan's trousers.

"Why don't you both say sorry to each other," Nan suggested.

"But she hurt me!" Tippi wailed.

"I'm sorry ... that you're such a baby," Ava said, getting to her feet. "Come on, Jack. Let's go."

"And where do you think you're off to?" Nan asked.

"Terry's house," Ava said. "I'll be with Jack, we'll be careful."

"Make up with Tippi first. I won't have you fighting. If you can't be nice to each other, I'll turn the boat around and take you both home to your mother."

"Sorry, Tippi," Ava said, sulkily.

"And you, Tippi," Nan prompted.

"Sorry, Ava," Tippi replied.

"I'll be back after dinner," Ava said, taking a pair of waterproof trousers from a hook by the door and pulling them on over her leggings. "We'll eat at Terry's."

"You don't have two spare carrier bags and a couple of elastic bands, do you?" Jack asked.

Nan pulled a couple of plastic bags from a drawer and handed them to him.

He put on his socks, then stepped into the bags. Taking elastic bands from a bowl of bits and bobs on the side, he used them to hold the bags around his feet and calves, before sliding them into his wet wellington boots.

"I want to go with them," Tippi muttered to Nan.

"I don't think that's a good idea, petal," Nan said softly, kissing the top of her head. "There's too much water out there. You and I can do some painting. How about we do some more bee-eaters?"

"See you later," Ava called out as they left. She set a brisk pace as they made their way back towards town.

"Terry's house is at the bottom of the hill that leads up to Twitch's. It will have been hit by the floodwater."

"If he's helping out at home, he might not be able to come with us."

"Maybe, but Terry has two older brothers, three older sisters and one younger sister. There are plenty of people to help out."

"Terry's one of seven?"

"Yeah. I think that's why he's so easy to get along with. He's difficult to upset, and he doesn't hold grudges," Jack said. "It's probably why he talks so much too. He has to, to be heard in his house. It makes sense him being best mates with Ozuru."

"Why?"

"Because Ozuru's chill. He's not competitive" – Jack paused – "and he thinks before he speaks."

"That's some pretty impressive detective work." Ava smiled at him. "You certainly aren't playing."

18

SKINNER'S MINIONS

"Count me in," Terry said, after Jack and Ava had told him that they wanted to eavesdrop on Nick Skinner's meeting. "Anything's got to be better than staying in this mad house."

The three of them were perching on the breakfast bar in Terry's kitchen. The lino floor was covered with about ten centimetres of water.

"Mum and Dad turned us into a human chain this morning so we could get all the furniture and stuff upstairs quickly," Terry said. "Everything is piled up in our bedrooms. Who knows where we're going to sleep? The place looks like a jumble sale. Mum keeps crying." He looked down at the kitchen floor and sighed. "Dad keeps going on about the house insurance and saying the car will be ruined." He looked at Jack. "He blames the toffs on the hill for burning the heather and drying out the land."

"That's what Reggie said."

"I daren't tell him I've got a job up there helping out at the party on Friday." Terry looked guilty.

"You don't have to do it," Jack said.

"I'm going to give Dad the money," Terry said, "and if it means we stop them from hurting that vulture, it's worth it." He looked at Jack. "Did you tell Twitch and the others? Together, we've got a better chance of stopping Nick Skinner."

"I tried." Jack shook his head. "Twitch laughed. He said it was impossible that someone would want to kill the bird, and that I was just playing at being a detective."

"He never!" Terry looked disbelieving. "Did you tell him about Lady Goremore and *that room*?"

"I didn't get a chance."

"Wow." Terry blinked with surprise. "I really thought he'd want to help."

"Let's see what we find out at six o'clock," Ava said. "We don't know for definite what Nick Skinner's planning. If we get some concrete evidence that he is hunting the bearded vulture, that will change Twitch's mind."

"We don't need Twitch," Jack said. "We're doing great on our own."

*　　*　　*

Jack, Ava and Terry decided to go to the playground behind St Mary's church, at the top of the high street, and sit on the swings. From there, they watched the world go by. They didn't know where Nick Skinner was going to meet Peaky, but Mord Hall was out on the west side of town, and Peaky lived on the east side. With most of the surrounding area being flooded, it stood to reason that wherever the meeting was, one of them was going to have to pass along the high street, either on foot or in a jeep.

Jack sat on the roundabout reading the chapter on vultures in the pocketbook. Terry and Ava were on the swings. He was telling her about Briddvale.

"If you go left off the high street, you get to our school. Past the school is the canal, and the old paper mill. Behind there is where Tara lives. Ozuru lives on this side of the school, closer to me. It takes me eight minutes to walk from my house to Ozuru's front door. I timed it once. It takes me longer to walk up the hill to Twitch's but I reckon that's because it's uphill all the way. I hate hills."

Ava laughed.

"That is Mr Bettany's, the local newsagent's. Twitch does a paper round for him at the weekend. Mr Bettany's a good sort. He'll give you a free chocolate bar if you can prove it's your birthday."

"What's he doing now?" Ava asked, as they watched the proprietor of the newsagent carrying box after box out of his shop and piling them up down a waterlogged side alley.

"Floodwater's got to his stock," Terry said mournfully, and they all took a moment to consider the tragedy of the loss of so many delicious sweets.

A gaggle of people were setting up giant tea and coffee urns on a trestle table outside the town hall. A truck arrived with camp beds and sleeping bags.

"The flood must have got some people really bad," Terry said, watching them unload.

"I wonder if many birdwatchers were planning to camp?" Ava said.

"Dad says the hotel and all the bed and breakfasts are full."

"It's them," Jack hissed, jumping up, then sitting back down again, trying to look casual. "It's Peaky and he's with Madden."

Terry and Ava kept swinging, watching Peaky and Madden sloshing down the high street, shoving and splashing one another. Everyone who saw them coming moved out of their way or crossed the road.

"They're not in any hurry," Ava said.

"What time is it?" Jack asked.

Terry looked at his watch. "Four forty-seven."

"We should follow them," Jack said, getting up.

"Let them get further ahead first," Terry said, nervously. "We don't want them to see us."

Once Peaky and Madden were at the end of the parade of shops, Jack, Ava and Terry left the playground, trying to look naturally nonchalant.

"They're going in the direction of Mord Hall," Jack observed.

As they got towards the edge of town, the buildings thinned and Jack felt more conspicuous, but he needn't have worried. It didn't cross the minds of the two lads in front that anyone would be following them. They didn't turn around.

Once they'd left Briddvale, the road developed an incline and the water got shallower until there was nothing but rivulets streaming down the hill. Jack suggested they leap the ditch beside the road, which had become a stream, and walk along behind the hedgerow so that, should Peaky and Madden turn around, they wouldn't be seen.

The field was very muddy, and all conversation stopped with the effort of walking through it without getting stuck or losing their balance.

"Look. There's Mord Hall." Jack pointed to the lit-up

house on the deep-blue horizon and they all realized it was getting dark.

"Um, got some bad news, guys," Terry said, poking his head over the hedge. "We've lost them."

"What?" Ava looked. "Where did they go? There is nowhere to go!"

Jack saw a pair of headlights crossing a field to the north of the one they were walking through. He pulled out his binoculars. "There." He passed the binoculars to Ava. "That's Nick Skinner's jeep."

"Let's go," Ava said, handing them back and marching off across the muddy field of corn stubble.

"Stay low and move quietly," Terry whispered.

As they approached the hedge at the top of the field, all three of them were walking in a crouch. Jack found a spot where the hedge was balding and squatted down to peer through. He saw the familiar figures of Peaky and Madden: one rangy, one burly; one with greasy hair, the other wearing a baseball cap backwards. Both in puffer jackets. They were shambling along a dirt track between the two fields with their shoulders hunched. Waiting for them, leaning against the tailgate of his jeep, was Nick Skinner.

Jack felt a shiver of fear at the sight of the man. He

put his hand down to shift his weight and immediately regretted the decision as it sank into sloppy mud.

When Peaky and Madden saw Nick Skinner they straightened up and developed a swagger.

"Get flooded out?" Nick asked his nephew.

"A bit." Peaky sniffed as he nodded.

"Your mother all right?"

"Says Dad's gonna have to buy her the new couch she's been asking for."

Nick snorted.

"Peaky says you've got a job for us?" Madden said.

Nick grunted. "Need you to bait some traps. Got a bird that needs killing."

"Urgh!" Peaky's head rocked back as he groaned like a child. "Why can't we just shoot it?"

"Because you'll miss," Nick replied flatly.

"Which bird is it?" Madden asked.

"What's it to you?"

"My dad says a lot of people have come to town to see a special bird."

"Did he now?"

"I don't want to get into any trouble," Madden said. "I'm in enough already."

"If we do this, can we go back to being loaders on the hunt?" Peaky asked.

Madden looked enquiringly at Nick, obviously keen.

"Can't trust you with guns until I know you will do as I say." Nick stared unblinking at the lads. "I've asked you to lay the traps."

"Why have we got to kill the bird?" Madden asked.

"It's dangerous," Nick replied.

"Dangerous? It's a bird!" Madden scoffed at the thought of a bird being a threat.

"Not to you, you idiot. Though if it took a disliking to you, you'd end up in a terrified bloody mess on the floor, I'd wager." Nick gave a guttural chuckle at this image. "The bird is dangerous to the sheep."

"Sheep?"

"It's called a lammergeier. Know what that means?"

Jack silently sucked in his breath. They *were* after the vulture!

Peaky and Madden shook their heads.

"It means *lamb killer*. The birds kill sheep. Eat 'em. Tear 'em apart."

"That's a lie!" Jack whispered, outraged. "Vultures don't kill…" Terry nudged him to shut up.

"There's a lot of sheep on the Mord Estate. I don't want that bloody great bird picking them off."

"Right. Got it." Peaky nodded. "Don't we?" He knocked his elbow against Madden's. "We're laying

176

the poisoned rabbit traps to kill the bird and protect the sheep."

"That's it. You're protecting sheep." A sly, unnerving smile crossed Nick Skinner's chapped lips. "There's a bag of dead rabbits in the back of the jeep." He pulled a box the size of a hardback book from his coat pocket and handed it to Peaky. "This is the stuff to put in 'em. You know what to do. Same as before."

"You want us to make a trail?"

"Looks like the bird'll be arriving in the next few days," Nick said, nodding. "Make sure the traps are down before then." He turned and climbed into his jeep, watching in his wing mirror as Madden retrieved a heavy-looking potato sack from the back, then he fired up the ignition.

Jack, Terry and Ava flattened themselves into the mud as the jeep did a three-point turn and drove away.

19
FRIGHTENED RABBITS

"When do you want to do it?" Madden asked Peaky, holding up the sack of dead rabbits.

"Not tonight," Peaky replied. "It's too wet."

"Tomorrow?"

"Yeah. We can camp out if the rain holds off."

Madden opened the sack and peered in, wrinkling his nose in disgust. "I ain't taking these home."

"Nor me this," Peaky said, shaking the box. "Mum'd freak if she found it in my room. Let's hide 'em here."

"We've got to come back this way anyhow," Madden agreed.

The two lads set about looking for a hiding place and Jack, Terry and Ava shrank back, fearful of being seen. If Peaky or Madden looked over the hedge, into the field, they'd be caught.

"There's a pothole here, under this spiky bush."

Madden was on the far side of the dirt track. He pulled the sleeve of his puffer coat over his hand, lifted the gorse, and shoved the sack into the hole.

"I can still see it," Peaky said, marching straight towards Jack's hiding place.

Flattening himself against the cold wet earth, Jack held his breath as his chin sank into the mud. Peaky squatted down on the other side of the hedge, directly opposite him. He reached under the bushes and gathered a mound of wet soil from in front of Jack's face. He stood up, carrying it over and dumping it on top of the sack. Madden stamped it down.

"Yeah. That's better." Peaky pulled a plastic bag from his coat pocket, put the box Nick had given him inside it, wrapped the bag around the box and slotted it into the bush. "Should keep it dry."

"Just looks like a bit of trash." Madden nodded at what he considered a job well done. "No one's going to come along here anyway. Everyone's busy clearing up the water."

"Let's go." Peaky wiped his muddy hands on his jacket and glanced over his shoulder, belatedly checking that no one was watching. "Want to go see if the snooker hall is open?"

"There's no electricity, dummy," Madden said,

striding away up the track. "The whole town's turned off because of the flooding."

"All right." Peaky hurried to fall in step beside him. "It was just a suggestion."

Jack, Terry and Ava watched them walk away.

"How long do you think we should wait before moving?" Terry whispered, his teeth juddering. "I'm freezing."

Ava sat up on her knees and stared after them. "I don't think they're coming back."

Once they were certain Peaky and Madden had gone, all three of them clambered over the hedge. Jack went to the gorse bush and pulled out the bag, opening it. "Rat poison," he whispered, pulling out the box so they could see the label. "Nick Skinner is getting Peaky and Madden to lay a trail of poisoned rabbits to lure the vulture down from the sky to feed."

"Pretty cowardly for the best shot in the country," Ava said, disgusted.

"He's using them, telling them the lammergeier will kill the sheep," Terry said, outraged. "My brothers do it to me. They get me to do something, telling me it'll please Mum, and when she finds out and is cross, I'm the one in hot water. She never believes that they put me up to it. That's what Nick Skinner's doing! If there's trouble, he'll blame Peaky and Madden for killing the bird, and if they get away with killing the bird, he'll take it to Lady Goremore."

"Sly fox," Ava said.

"That's what he meant about *'being clever'*." Jack nodded.

"Peaky and Madden are too stupid to realize they're being set up," Terry said.

"He's getting them to do his dirty work," Jack agreed, "but the blood is on his hands."

"And Lady Goremore's," Ava added, grimly. "She's the one that wants it stuffed and put in a case."

"What should we do?" Terry looked down despairingly at his muddy front.

"We can't let them put rat poison in dead rabbits." Jack gestured to the fields around them. "Anything could eat it! Lots of animals feed on … carrion." He'd never used that word before. It surprised him when it came out of his mouth, but he knew it meant dead animals. Twitch had taught him that.

"Well?" Ava looked at Jack expectantly. "What are we going to do?"

"Let me think."

Careful not to rip it, Jack prised the top of the cardboard box open. Inside was a sealed plastic bag.

He lifted it up between muddy thumb and forefinger. The poison was little turquoise granules.

"Looks like Toxic Fizzy Drops," Terry said, with a startled laugh.

"Those sweets that come in plastic TNT tubs?" Ava nodded. "Yeah. You're right. The blueberry flavoured ones."

Jack stared at the bag of poison. It did look like sweets. "Mr Bettany sells Toxic Fizzy Drops ... and he was dumping boxes of ruined sweets out in the alley beside the shop." A plan began to form in his head. "What if we swapped the poison for sweets?"

Terry's and Ava's expressions became gleeful as they caught on to his idea. "Yes!"

"OK, here's the plan." Jack pulled the bag of turquoise granules out of the box and returned the empty box in the bag to its hiding place. "Terry, tomorrow morning, go and salvage as many packets of blueberry Toxic Fizzy Drops from Mr Bettany's boxes as possible. They're inside plastic tubs so the water shouldn't have got to them. Take them home and empty them into a sandwich bag, one of those ones your mum puts your packed lunch in. We need it to look as close to this as possible." He held up the bag of poison.

"Got it." Terry nodded. "I can cut off the fastening

strip, add a thin line of superglue, hairdryer it and turn it upside down in the box. It'll look the same."

"Great. When it's ready, you need to come back here and put it into the empty box." Jack pointed at the gorse bush.

"What about the poison?" Ava asked, staring at the bag.

"That's your job," Jack replied. "You are going to have to find some way of getting rid of it that won't harm any animals."

"Can't bury it," Ava mused as she took the bag. "If I throw it away, it could still get eaten, by a fox or something."

"What about burning it?" Jack suggested. "You've got a wood-burning stove on the *Kingfisher*."

"What if it explodes? Or makes a poison gas?" Ava shook her head. "I don't think Nan would be happy with me if I put it in the stove."

"There's a toxic waste disposal skip at the dump. My dad put our old car battery in there," Terry said. "It's on the other side of town, just before the Rosefinch Marina. You could fling it in there."

"Great idea. I'll do it tomorrow morning when the dump opens." Ava turned to Jack. "You look serious. What are you thinking?"

"To catch these guys we'll need evidence to show the police," Jack said. "Getting that will be my job."

"It will be easier if we tell the others, and get their help, now that we know Nick Skinner's plan," Terry said.

Jack knew Terry didn't like having secrets from Ozuru, but he shook his head. "Not yet." He wanted Twitch to see that detecting wasn't a childish game. It was important. Jack might not be good at watching birds, but he was going to save one, and not just any bird either, a lammergeier. Then his friend would feel bad that he thought it was a stupid game. Twitch would understand why Jack had done everything he'd done. He would forgive him for lying and apologize for laughing at him. Twitch would see that Jack *was* a good detective.

If he saved the bearded vulture, he'd be a hero.

20

NIGHT STALKER

The next morning the sky mocked the memory of yesterday by being icy blue and cloudless. A skittish wind caused the standing water in the street to wrinkle, and Jack could see the flood level going down.

Yesterday, his parents had got most of the water out of the house using pumps. There were sandbags stacked around the front and back doors, to stave off the flood, but there was still no electricity or heating to dry anything out. Jack's home smelled like his football socks when he'd shoved them in a plastic bag and forgotten about them after a rainy match.

His mum had been very upset by his disappearing trick yesterday, and she was even more unhappy about his returning after dark, sopping wet, covered in mud. Jack was told off for nearly an hour. His parents had gone on and on about how worried they'd been, how reckless it was of him to go off in his friend's boat when they thought he was only going to the end of the road. He'd apologized several times and said he'd never do it again and eventually his mum had calmed down, but only after producing a list of chores she expected him to complete today. Then she had sent him to his room.

Later, his dad had brought up a plate of food – a random assortment of cold things from the cupboards: a roll, crackers, slices of cheese, salami, an apple and a pickled onion. He'd called it a ploughman's dinner and told Jack that he understood his desire for adventure, however, he'd been selfish to make his mum worry. He'd winked as he left, and Jack knew he wasn't in serious trouble.

Winnie had kept Jack company as he'd eaten his ploughman's dinner and read the book about vultures that he'd taken from the *Kingfisher*. He'd been surprised to find it was interesting. By the end of the book Jack had decided that vultures really were cool. People thought them ghastly and gruesome, but they were much misunderstood. "When the zombie apocalypse comes, Winnie, I'm going to get a pet vulture," Jack had said, tearing off a bit of salami and feeding it to the dog. "I'm going to call it … Gorgon. When I set it on the undead, it'll tear off their arms and eat them. I love you, but you need to understand, vultures are the best pet for an apocalypse."

Today Jack only had one thing on his mind. He hadn't told Ava and Terry in case they tried to talk him out of it, but tonight he planned to follow Peaky and Madden as they set their poison traps. Terry had messaged him to say he'd planted the sweets, and Ava had sent a message saying she'd managed to dispose of the poison safely. He'd replied telling them he was grounded, but had a plan to get the evidence they needed, and to trust him.

Jack did his chores with cheerful gusto, glad to have something to make the time pass before tonight's adventure. He helped his dad photograph the wallpaper in each room downstairs, recording the level the water had risen to with a ruler, noting down damage for the insurance claim. He'd scrubbed the floors with his mum, to try and rid the house of its new pungent smell.

"I wish we had gas or electricity," his mother said as they scrubbed. "One would do. I don't mind which. I've half a mind to attend the town hall meeting just to get a decent cup of tea."

Jack smiled and was lovely and helpful all day. When he'd completed his mum's list of tasks, he asked what more he could do.

Dinner was spaghetti hoops on toast that his dad cooked on a camping stove hooked up to a Calor Gas canister, borrowed from a neighbour.

"Mum, I was wondering," Jack said, as they ate their spaghetti hoops. "Would you mind if I stayed at Twitch's tonight? I know you're cross with me about yesterday, but Twitch sent me a message saying his electricity and heating has come back on. His house is on the north side of town and wasn't flooded. He says I can have a bath if I stay over."

"Oh, I'd love a nice hot bubble bath right now." His mother sighed, closing her eyes and picturing it.

"So would I." Jack held his breath.

"Oh, go on then." His mum ruffled his hair. "You've been really helpful today and you're as mucky as sin. You could do with a wash. We all could."

"Thanks, Mum." Jack beamed. "I'll ask Mrs Featherstone if you and Dad can go over for a bath tomorrow if you like?"

"I can't give you a lift," his dad said. "The car isn't working. I think it might be dead."

"I can walk. I'll go along the Briddvale Road and take a torch. If I get my stuff straight after dinner, I can be there by six thirty."

"I'll walk with you into town," his dad said, after

a glance from his mother. "I'll see if I can find out when we're likely to get the power back."

Jack ran upstairs and got changed into thermal base layers under black combat trousers and two long-sleeved T-shirts. He put on a thin jumper and a fleece underneath his coat. He'd decided on walking boots with thick socks because his wellies were still wet inside, and the water was no longer knee-deep if he stuck to the roads. He loaded his trouser pockets with gloves, a torch, binoculars, a stubby foldaway umbrella, a folded carrier bag, his notebook and pen, a couple of energy bars, and his phone, which was fully charged.

He walked with his dad up the Briddvale Road into town, waved goodbye at the turning for Twitch's road, then hid for a minute and shadowed his father all the way to the town hall. Once his dad had gone inside, Jack ran, only slowing down once he was out the other side of town.

When he got to the dirt track where they'd spied on Peaky and Madden yesterday, Jack went to the gorse bush hiding the dead rabbits and pulled out the box of rat poison. He opened it and lifted out the plastic bag. Terry had done an expert job. The sweets didn't look exactly the same as the poison, but they bore a close enough resemblance. If you weren't an expert –

and Jack hoped that Peaky and Madden weren't – you wouldn't know there'd been a switch.

He scouted around for a sheltered hiding place where he could settle down and wait. At a junction where one hedgerow met another, a bit further up the trail, there was a badger-sized hole. He pulled up enough green foliage to hide behind, then laid his carrier bag down on the ground to prevent his trousers from getting damp, and settled in to wait. He thought about playing on his phone, but he didn't want to use up the battery. He needed it to collect photographic evidence of Peaky and Madden making poison rabbit traps and, if possible, record audio of them talking about Nick Skinner and their evil mission.

As time ticked on, Jack became restless. He didn't know when Peaky and Madden would turn up. He could be sitting here for hours.

He thought about how impressed Twitch would be when he found out that Jack had saved the lammergeier, and suddenly he realized what he could do whilst he waited. He took out his binoculars, notebook and pen. The notebook hadn't completely dried out from the soaking it had got on the ride home from Mord Hall. He was glad he'd written in biro. Lifting his binoculars, Jack scoured the sky above Rooky Wood for nocturnal birds.

As night deepened, he chased the calls of hooting owls, but failed to spot one. A full moon lit up the horizon and Jack wondered why he hadn't notice it rise. Twitch often told him he was in too much of a hurry, to slow down if he wanted to see things, and Jack knew there was truth in this.

Translucent clouds, like tattered moth wings, sailed across the sky occasionally, but it was a clear and cold night. It seemed as if all the stars had turned out to watch the evening's drama.

Being a fan of horror films had its downsides when you had time to kill. Having an overactive imagination whilst you were sitting on a hillside at night, waiting for two lads who'd beaten you up to collect a bag of dead rabbits and a box of rat poison, was punishing.

Jack tried to think about other things but found himself wondering where Nick Skinner had got his bag of dead rabbits from. Had he shot them? An image sprang into Jack's head of steel traps with jagged teeth, and Nick Skinner smashing a trapped bunny over the head with a rock. The shadows took on the form of the surly gamekeeper and Jack began to wish Peaky and Madden would hurry up just so that he wouldn't be alone out here. The wind in the grass sounded like the gamekeeper's rasping breath. Every noise made

Jack jump. What if Nick Skinner was walking the land tonight? What if he was watching Peaky and Madden? Jack had better be on his guard.

It was nearly ten o'clock when Jack heard laughter. He clicked off his torch, slipping it into his pocket. A few minutes later bobbing lights, like two giddy fireflies, crested the hill and bounded towards him. Peaky and Madden strode along the dirt track, each wearing a beanie with a head torch strapped to it and carrying a rucksack.

Jack watched them retrieve the sack and the rat poison. It was too dark for them to see that the box had been tampered with.

"Peeyew! These rabbits stink." Madden recoiled after opening the sack and peering inside.

Jack waited until they'd climbed the gate, setting off over the field towards Rooky Wood, before moving aside the branches he'd propped in front of his hiding place. He folded the carrier bag he'd been sitting on, then as carefully and quietly as he could, he set out after them.

It was much easier to shadow the two lads than he'd thought it would be. It didn't occur to them that they weren't alone in the world. They talked and joked loudly, laughing when one of them tripped or got spooked by a creature in the grass.

"This is the beginning of the Mord Estate." Peaky pointed to a fence. "On the other side is Rooky Wood."

Jack crept closer, making sure his phone was on silent, then turned on the recorder and held it out in front of him.

"Should we put a rabbit out here, to encourage the vulture bird this way?"

"How many do we have in the bag?"

"Four."

"We need one for the rocks by Passerine Pike, one for the track that leads up to it…"

"If we put one here the bag will be lighter," Madden said.

"If we put one here, and people who aren't from the Mord Estate find it, we could be in big trouble."

"Then let's dump one on the other side of the fence."

"Uncle Nick said it's got to be where there are no trees, so the vulture can see it."

"You carry the sack then." Madden thrust the bag at Peaky. "They stink. You can put on the rat poison too. It's gross."

"If I'm doing the baiting" – Peaky shoved the sack back at Madden – "then you can carry the bag. Or else why are you here?"

Madden reluctantly grunted his agreement, then the two lads helped each other over the waist-high barbed-wire fence.

Jack felt a spark of glee at capturing this bit of conversation. He stopped the recorder, hoping Peaky and Madden had been loud enough for their words to be clear.

After the lads had walked into Rooky Wood, Jack turned his attention to the fence. He knew Ava would have run at it, leaned on the wooden post, and scissored her legs over in a second. He wasn't sure that he could clear it, and barbed wire could give you a nasty scratch where you really didn't want one.

Putting on his gloves, he selected the baggiest bit of barbed wire and yanked it up, pushing the wire below it down. Stepping one leg into the gap, he carefully wiggled his bottom and dipped his head through, adjusted his balance and brought through his remaining leg with a sigh of relief. Straightening up, he turned to Rooky Wood and his heart lurched. He couldn't see or hear Peaky and Madden. He scanned the trees. He wasn't even certain which direction they'd gone in.

It was dark in Rooky Wood. Jack'd not been there before. He didn't know where the paths were and couldn't risk turning on his torch. A ripple of panic twisted his stomach. He calmed himself with a deep breath. What would Twitch do? He closed his eyes and stood, quietly, listening to the woods. After a couple of long minutes, Jack heard the alarmed call of wood pigeons woken from their sleep. He opened his eyes and saw a bird shoot up out of the canopy, making a brief silhouette against the milky moon. He smiled and headed in that direction.

Rooky Wood was a thick phalanx of trees separating the manicured grounds of Mord Hall from the heath of the grouse moors. Peaky and Madden marched through the wood and out the other side, into the springy heather and bracken of the moor.

Jack tracked them, keeping to the fringe of the wood, using tree shadows as cover.

As they crossed the open land, the moon shone a sepia spotlight on Peaky and Madden. Jack could see them clearly. They stopped and bent down.

"You're so squeamish!" Peaky teased, laughing.

Madden turned away. He was gagging, like he was going to throw up.

Jack heard the rattle of the box of rat poison. They were setting the first trap. He slid his phone from his pocket and crept towards them. As he zoomed in to take a photo, the screen blazed with light. Jack panicked, fumbling the phone and dropping it. Throwing himself on the ground, he grabbed the phone and shoved it into his pocket.

"What was that?" Madden asked Peaky.

"All I could hear was you puking."

"Shut up! I didn't puke!" He looked around. "I heard something."

"Could've been grouse? A fox maybe, or a badger?" Peaky replied nonchalantly. "Not getting scared, are you?" He paused and then said in a nasty voice. "It could be my Uncle Nick, following us to make sure we're doing a proper job."

Madden straightened at this. "Quit your messing. I'm just saying I thought I heard something. That's all."

"Who's going to be up here, on private land, at eleven o'clock at night?" Peaky said. "It's the Mord Estate. No one's allowed here." He left another pause. "Except my uncle..."

Madden shoved him and Peaky laughed.

"We've done one," Madden said.

"Three to go," Peaky added. "Come on."

As they tramped off across the moor, Jack allowed himself a smile. Peaky and Madden had left a dead rabbit on the ground covered in harmless sweets. The plan was working.

21

SHOOTING BUTT

As the moor rose in front of him, Jack's confidence grew. Peaky and Madden were clearly visible as they followed a narrow path up the hill, their head torches acting like lighthouse beacons. He'd have plenty of time to drop if either of them turned around, and because he wasn't using a light, his eyes were well-adjusted to the dark.

Looming up beyond the two lads was Passerine Pike: the tallest hill in a long range north of Briddvale. It had a distinctive rock formation at its peak. It looked as though the stones had burst out of the ground like a broken bone might split skin. A winding footpath, a public right of way, led from a car park at the bottom all the way to the top. It was a common walk for ramblers who wanted to admire the view across the valley. Jack's parents had dragged him up it when they'd first moved to Briddvale in the spring. Twitch had brought him up it to watch starling murmurations in the early autumn but he'd never been up on his own.

Between Passerine Pike and the Mord lands was a high wooden and barbed-wire fence, through which weaved an old hedgerow tangled with thorny blackberry runners and nettles. Every few metres there was a yellow sign telling people on the outside that the inside was private land, and that trespassers would be prosecuted. In the late summer a new sign had appeared, warning ramblers that from the twelfth of August till the end of December, grouse shooting took place on the other side of the fence.

"In other words," Twitch had said, "if you come on our land, we'll sue you or shoot you."

Jack ducked as Peaky and Madden stopped to set another bunny trap. He snuck forwards, silently photographing them as they laid the unfortunate rabbit on the path. Jack was praying the moonlight was bright enough for it to be clear in the picture what it was they were doing.

They set the third trap on an outcrop of rocks. Jack was mildly impressed by their choice of location. It was a place where you could imagine a bearded vulture might break the bones of its breakfast. The area looked like a bird of prey feeding station, although he guessed very few birds of prey lingered in the skies over Mord Hall.

"We've got one left," Madden said, holding up the bag.

"We'll put it near the shooting butt."

"Is that where we're going to camp?"

"Yeah."

"Are we close? 'Cause I'm knackered."

"It's up there, near the Pike." Peaky took the bag from him. "I'll bait the last rabbit if you make camp. Just throw the tarpaulin over the top of the shooting butt and weigh it down with stones."

"All right. Are you going to put that rabbit somewhere we can see from the door?"

"Yeah, and when the vulture comes, *kapow, kapow, kapow,*" Peaky made shooting sounds. "It'll be a sitting duck."

"A duck?"

"An easy target." Peaky swung his rucksack off his shoulder and patted a dark parcel strapped to the back. "Guess who nicked their uncle's air rifle from his gun cabinet?"

"You never?" Madden sounded impressed. "I brought my slingshot, but a gun is way better."

"Shooting those cats was just for practice. This is the real thing. We're proper hunters now. We need a real weapon."

Jack's blood ran cold. This wasn't part of the plan. *They weren't meant to shoot the vulture!* He was so horrified by what they were saying, he forgot to record the conversation.

"We'll show Uncle Nick that we know how to handle a gun." Peaky leaped about pretending to shoot things. "He only said we should use poison after I tried to shoot that pigeon with your slingshot and missed."

"You missed?" Madden laughed.

"Shut up. Pigeons are way smaller than vultures!" Peaky protested.

"You are a rubbish shot."

"I'm not. I'm better than you. I'm the one that killed that cat. I'm going to be a marksman like my uncle."

"I never miss when I'm using my fists." Madden shadow-boxed the air.

"Yeah, but shooting is a skill."

"So is knocking out an opponent with one punch." Madden playfully punched Peaky's shoulder.

"Ouch! Stop it or…"

"Or you'll do what?" Madden punched him again, a bit harder this time.

"I'll throw this dead rabbit at you." Peaky reached into the bag and pulled out the last bunny by its ears.

"Man, you are sick." Madden dropped his fists and turned away, walking towards the shooting butt. "When is the lamb killer arriving?"

"In the next few days, Uncle Nick said. Could be tomorrow or the next day."

Jack stayed where he was, watching Peaky lay the last trap. He took photos of him sprinkling the Toxic Fizzy Drops over the rabbit, but all the while his mind was whirring.

When he was done, Peaky climbed the hill to help his partner in crime, who was wrestling with a sheet of tarpaulin. The shooting butt was a circular shelter, built from a dry-stone wall, sunk into the ground, with a door-sized gap as an entrance. Turf lined the top of the wall, where grouse hunters would rest the barrels of their guns. As they set up their camp, Jack stared at the air rifle strapped to Peaky's rucksack.

I need to get that gun.

Once they'd anchored down the tarp, making a roof for their camp, Peaky and Madden dragged their bags inside and built a fire in front of the doorway.

Jack shivered as he looked on, envious of the warmth from their fire. He hadn't planned on spending the night under the stars. He'd thought he'd get his evidence and creep home, to his own bed, telling his parents that he'd fallen out with Twitch. He hadn't brought any shelter or bedding. He stared up at the star-freckled sky. The lammergeier wouldn't be poisoned, but that would mean nothing if Peaky shot the bird with an air rifle.

I'll wait until they fall asleep, Jack thought. Then I'll creep into their camp and steal the gun. If Peaky doesn't have a gun, he can't shoot the vulture.

Then he remembered the slingshot and realized he was going to have to steal that too.

Jack wished he'd told Ava and Terry what he was doing. He'd feel better if someone knew where he was. He thought about sending them a message and took out his phone. It was past midnight, they'd be asleep, but at least they'd see his message in the morning. The screen lit up and his heart sank as he saw the signal bars were at zero. He was on his own.

22

SKYWATCH HIDE

"I'm gutted we don't get to go trick-or-treating this year," Madden said, poking a stick in the fire.

"Yeah, but we'll earn good money at the Halloween Ball," Peaky pointed out.

"It's not as much fun as lying in wait for little kids, scaring the hell out of them and stealing their sweets." Madden gave a low guttural laugh.

"What was that?" Peaky grabbed Madden's wrist as the dark night was pierced by the long harsh screech of a barn owl.

Twitch had taught Jack the calls of nocturnal birds. For the first time Jack understood what Twitch meant about feeling like the birds were his companions. He found the barn owl's hunting cry thrilling because he recognized what it was, and he smiled to see how it scared Peaky and Madden.

"The fire will keep wild animals from attacking us," Madden said, obviously shaken. "They hate fire. They're scared of it."

Jack pushed his lips together, swallowing a laugh. Considering these were the two meanest bullies in Briddvale, he was surprised and delighted that every hoot, squawk or rustle made them jump. He wondered what wild animals they thought lived on the heath. There were no lions in Briddvale.

Moving away from the camp, Jack found a flat outcrop of rock and walked back and forth, as quietly as possible, wrapping his arms around himself and bouncing on his toes to keep warm. The temperature was dropping. His breath was a tell-tale white mist and he fancied he could see frost forming on the bracken. He needed somewhere to shelter until Peaky and Madden fell asleep.

Passerine Pike loomed over him and, as Jack stared up at it, it occurred to him that somewhere over there, nestled among the rocks, was the skywatch hide. If he could find it in the dark, it would shelter him from the elements. He could watch the shooting butt through his binoculars and come back when he was sure Peaky and Madden were asleep. They'd have to put the fire out when they went to bed, which would be a clear sign.

Jack strode eagerly up the hill towards the fence that kept the public off the Mord Estate. As he approached it, he could see that climbing over wasn't going to be easy. There were loops of barbed wire woven through the dense foliage and it was taller than Jack. He wondered how Ava would approach this one.

He walked along until he found a fence post with a flat square of wood screwed to it. It was one of the yellow warning signs that had gone up over the summer saying: *CAUTION! GROUSE SHOOTING IN PROGRESS ON THIS MOOR TODAY.* Jack jumped but he couldn't quite reach it. He risked pulling his torch from his pocket and turning it on. He studied the tangle of hedge, fence panel and barbed wire, until he found the stub of a branch that looked like it might hold his weight. He stepped his left foot onto it and jumped, throwing his right arm up around the sign, then scrambled his feet, trying to walk up the fence. He heard the sign splitting, and, before he fell backwards, he launched himself forward with all his might over the top.

Barbed wire tore his trousers as he landed on his side with a thud that emptied his lungs of air. He felt a fresh pain as the skin on his face flamed with agony. As he struggled to get up, the grouse shooting sign hit him on the back of the head. He tumbled away from the fence, gasping for breath, unsure where to rub as everywhere hurt. He looked back and shone his torch at the fence. He'd fallen face first into a bed of stinging nettles.

It's just bruises and stings, Jack told himself, getting to his feet. The pain was mollified by the fact that he immediately felt safer, knowing he was on public land and there was a fence between him and the bullies with the air rifle. Trying to ignore his stinging face and bruised ribs, he staggered towards the towering outcrop of rock at the top of Passerine Pike.

Twitch always said that the key to a good hide was that it must be invisible. Jack cursed as he searched the rocks for the entrance. If only he'd come up with the others on Monday morning, he'd know where it was … but then he wouldn't have found out about the plot to kill the vulture.

Passerine Pike looked different in the dark. Shadows were longer, rocks seemed bigger, more imposing. They took on a character he'd not noticed by day. He felt like he was in an ancient, sacred place. Stumbling round and round the base of the rock formation, he became alarmed. He could find no sign of the skywatch hide. He fell to his knees and rested his forehead on a big boulder.

"Please help me," he whispered to the rocks. "I'm trying to save the lammergeier."

Lifting his head to look at the moon, he was about to make the same plea when he spotted the fringed edge of Ozuru's camouflage netting. Jack scrambled up onto the big boulder and there it was, a gap at his feet the size of a manhole cover, between two enormous rocks. He shone his torch into it and saw a wall of canvas with a zip down the middle. The skywatch hide! He felt a thrill as he lowered the zip and squirmed inside.

Jack sat down, enjoying the absence of icy breeze on his face, although his nettle stings buzzed angrily as he warmed up. There was a roll mat on the ground of the tent, and a couple of old cushions. Inside a plastic laundry bag, he found a blanket, a flask of water, a bigger torch, a stack of books and a first-aid kit. Jack spent a few minutes covering his face with sting cream, then he ate one of his energy bars, took a swig of water and wrapped himself in the blanket. After enjoying a few minutes of rest, he poked his head out of the tent, stretching up through the gap in the boulders.

Passerine Pike was on higher ground than the shooting butt. He should be able to see it through his binoculars. He rested his elbows on the rock and trained them on the Mord Estate. It didn't take him long to spot the blaze of the campfire. He could make out the silhouettes of two heads. They were still awake.

He slipped back inside the tent and zipped it up. His phone said it was ten minutes to one. He'd wait half an hour then check on them again. He moved the cushions, making himself comfy in a sitting position. He was dreading the return journey over that fence, but with the slingshot, he'd have the evidence he needed to get Peaky and Madden arrested for shooting Colonel Mustard, Splatty and the other cats. He'd got the recording and the photographs to prove they were trying to poison the bearded vulture, and if he could grab that gun and run, he would've saved the lammergeier.

He smiled as he imagined the reactions of the other Twitchers. Twitch would be so sorry for doubting him. He'd have to eat his words.

Jack's eyes drooped closed but he snapped them open, sucking in a breath.

I mustn't fall asleep.

He picked up one of the books on the lammergeier and read by torchlight, but barely ten minutes had passed when his head lolled forward.

Shaking himself, Jack slapped his cheeks, blinked madly, and drank more water.

I have to stay awake.

He looked at his phone. It had seventy per cent battery. He could risk using up a bit on playing a game to stay awake. He opened his favourite skateboard game, where you used your fingers to jump your way over an assault course. He told himself he could play for ten minutes and then he'd check on Peaky and Madden.

23

RASPBERRY ALERT

When Jack woke up, he was still clutching his phone, and light was streaming through the roof of the tent.

"NO! No, no, no, no!" Jack exclaimed, shoving the phone in his pocket as he jumped up, dropping the blanket, disorientated by sleep and panic. He didn't know what time it was.

His midnight plan had exploded into dust in the sunlight.

Was he too late? Was the lammergeier already dead?

Hurling himself out of the shelter, he scrambled onto the rocks and trained his binoculars on Peaky and Madden's camp. He gulped in big breaths of air, trying to calm down. "There it is." He scanned the area but saw no signs of life. The fire was out. The sun was low in the sky and a haze of pink sat behind the streaky grey clouds. "Sun's rising," he said, to calm himself, wrapping an arm across his chest, suddenly aware of how bitterly cold the morning was. "It's OK. It's still early."

Zipping up the tent behind him, Jack clambered down the rocks. Every minute that passed sent the sun higher into the sky, making it more likely that Peaky and Madden would wake up. If he wanted to get that gun, he was going to have to do it now!

He jogged to the fence. His muscles were stiff and ached from last night's adventures. In the rosy light of dawn, he could see where he'd hurled himself over the top last night. He marvelled that he wasn't more injured. He remembered that he still had an energy bar left in his pocket and ate it as he walked along the fence. With the benefit of daylight and higher ground, he found an easier way over the top and managed to climb the fence without injuring himself further.

Keeping low, he ran directly to Peaky and Madden's camp, ready to drop into the heather should he catch a peep of either of them.

Approaching from the rear, Jack tiptoed round to the doorway. The ashes of last night's fire were cold and damp. He pricked up his ears, listening for the rustle of movement or a murmur that suggested either of them was awake. He heard a droning sound and smiled, relaxing a little as he recognized snoring.

Jack crept to the doorway. It was dark. He could see feet in sleeping bags. He dropped to all fours and poked his head inside, his chest over the ashes of last night's fire. If either Peaky or Madden opened their eyes now, he'd immediately be seen.

He held his breath as his eyes adjusted, making out the sleeping figures of the two lads. Peaky was snoring. Madden was on his side, his back to his friend, his arm wrapped around his head. Each had their rucksacks beside them. Jack spotted the slingshot on the floor near the door and beside it the box of rat poison. He reached in and snatched the slingshot, stuffing it into his trouser pocket. Nick Skinner's air rifle was lying on the ground between the sleeping lads.

Jack drew back, breathing in great gulps of air. If he was quick and silent, he could dart in, grab the gun, and run.

They won't wake up, he told himself. If they do wake up, they'll be in their sleeping bags. They won't know what's happening. They'll be confused. I'll have a head start. I can outrun them.

Looking down the hill at Rooky Wood, Jack thought he could make it there and find somewhere to hide, before Peaky and Madden could catch up with him.

He scanned the horizon and saw no sign of the

bearded vulture. Jack's heart was racing. It was now or never.

All you have to do, he told himself, is dart in, grab the gun, get out and run.

He moved into the doorway, his feet planted either side of the extinguished fire, his body rigid with fear.

Dart in. Grab gun. Run.

Dart in. Grab gun. Run.

Jack lightly stepped over the fire pit. He took a small step forward. Then another. The gun was barely a metre away. He froze as Peaky groaned in his sleep and shifted his position. Jack's heart did a drum roll, but Peaky's rhythmic snoring resumed. Silently releasing his breath, Jack sank into a crouch, walking his hands across the frigid, compacted earth, inching towards the gun. Reaching out, he got one hand on the wooden handle of the weapon, his fingers curling around it. Carefully, he lifted it off the ground, drawing it back towards his body.

Madden stirred, shifting his legs and released a rip-roaring raspberry of a fart!

Jack's eyes snapped wide in shock at the sound.

Peaky's eyes sprang open.

Jack pivoted in a panic, leaping over the extinguished campfire.

"HEY! Stop! Thief!" Peaky yelled.

Run! Run! Run! Jack's brain screamed as he scissored his legs. The treacherously dewy ground betrayed him. His foot skidded. He tried to recover his balance. He felt a hand grab hold of his coat. Grass hurtled towards his face. Throwing his arms forward to stop his fall, his mind screamed that he was clutching a gun. He tried to fling it away. As he felt the walloping impact of his body hitting the earth, the gun skidded across the ground, blasting a shot across the field, decapitating seed heads.

A cawing chorus of alarm sounded as a scattering of winged silhouettes flushed from the distant trees, dark angels against a pale sky.

24

TOXIC FIZZY DEATH

"Get off!" Jack shouted as hands grabbed his ankles. He kicked his legs as he was yanked backwards. He grasped at frosty grass stalks, panic blazing in his chest, as he was dragged back to the shooting butt. His fleece rode up, the cold ground scraping against his stomach. Jack's chin hit a stone and he gritted his teeth as his face crashed into the stinking ash of the extinguished campfire.

"Well, what have we here?" The nasty nasal tone of Peaky was imitating a police officer. "Looks like we've caught a petty criminal."

"Dear oh dear, Richie," Madden chuckled. "He's going to have to be punished." He kicked Jack's thigh hard, and Jack stifled a cry, grateful the bully hadn't had time to put his boots on. "What should we do with him?"

215

"Depends." Peaky pulled on his trainers. "We need to keep an eye out for that bird. We don't want to miss our chance."

Jack rolled over and tried to sit up, hoping he could try to talk his way out of this, but Peaky kicked his chest and he found himself flat on his back and struggling to breathe.

"Let's tie him up," Peaky suggested. "I brought nylon cord to bind the dead bird once we shot it. We can use it on him instead."

"Nice." Madden gave Jack a smile that made his insides whimper. It was a promise of the beating to come.

Each hooking a hand under Jack's armpits, they threw him through the doorway of the shooting butt. He landed on Madden's red sleeping bag. Madden put his foot on Jack's chest while Peaky pulled a bundle of blue nylon rope from his rucksack.

"Listen, guys, you don't need to tie me up." Jack tried to sound calm and reasonable. "I'm not going anywhere."

"Too right you're not," Madden growled.

"You're trespassing. This is private property. What are you doing sneaking about here?" Peaky said. "My uncle's the gamekeeper of Mord Hall, you know? I'm going to enjoy handing you over to him."

"You casing the manor?" Madden asked. "Thief!"

"No! Of course I wasn't! I was, er, camping at Passerine Pike. I heard there was an amazing vulture coming this way. I was hoping to see it. It's a really rare bird, you know?" As Jack talked, his eyes frantically swept the shooting butt for anything that might help him out of his predicament. The ground was dug down and flattened. A stone bench lined the wall, for sitting on when loading a gun he supposed, or standing on to shoot the birds flushed out from the moor. The box of rat poison was just beyond his feet.

"Where's your gun?" Madden asked Peaky, as he tied Jack's ankles together.

"Outside on the ground." Peaky shot Jack an evil look. "That's what the rat was stealing, my uncle's gun." He leered at Jack. "Uncle Nick is not going to be pleased when I tell him you stole his air rifle. You haven't met my uncle. He's not the kind of man you want to upset."

"Want me to go get it?"

Peaky nodded.

Jack wracked his brains. He had to do something fast! He couldn't let them tie him up. He'd never get away. Madden was just outside the door. Peaky was stronger than Jack and, right now, tying his ankles together.

His thumping heart banged about in his chest like an angry bull in a confined space.

Think, Jack! Think!

"Richie! Richie!" Madden called out, sounding excited. "Check it out. There's a massive bird high up in the sky. Do you think it's that lamb killer one?"

Jack looked to the door, trying to see the bird. Peaky leaped to his feet, grabbing a pair of binoculars from the top of his open rucksack, knocking the bag over in his hurry to get outside. The falling rucksack hit the box of rat poison. Terry's blueberry Toxic Fizzy Drops spilled across the red sleeping bag.

Jack had to do something, *right now*! He wouldn't be able to live with himself if Peaky or Madden hurt a feather on that vulture's body. Suddenly Jack became incredibly calm and focused. That was it! If they wanted to hurt the lammergeier, they were going to have to do it over his dead body.

As Peaky scrambled out the doorway, Jack wriggled towards the Toxic Fizzy Drops. He reached his hand into his trouser pocket, pulled out his phone and clicked on the audio recorder.

"YES! That's it!" Peaky shrieked. "That's the lamb killer. Wow! It's massive."

"Do you think it's seen the rabbit?" Madden sounded excited. "Go on, birdy, eat the yummy bunny."

"Quick! Give me the gun. There's no way I'm gonna

miss that!" Peaky was beside himself. "GAH! It needs reloading."

The pair of them tumbled back into the shooting butt, ignoring Jack. Peaky grabbed his rucksack, pulling everything out in his hurry to get ammunition for the gun.

"Are you ready then?" Jack asked cheerily.

"Ready for what?" Peaky didn't even look at him as he pulled out a box of pellets from his bag.

"To punish me," Jack replied, smiling. "To beat me up or at least, to attempt to hurt me."

"You *want* us to hit you?" Madden said from the doorway.

"I'd like to see you try." Jack lifted his chin in challenge. "You're all mouth and no trousers, you two."

"Leave him," Peaky said, putting the pellets into the gun. "We'll beat him up after we've shot that vulture. Uncle Nick's going to be so pleased with me."

"Yeah, Tommy, you do as Richie tells you, there's a good little boy," Jack said, grinning. He could see Madden was itching to punch him. "I'll just sit here and wait shall I, till he gives you permission to come back?"

"You got a death wish or something?" Madden said.

"Maybe I have!" Jack looked around. "Do you know, I haven't had any breakfast yet and I'm starving. I might just eat your sweets," he said, grabbing a fistful of Toxic Fizzy Drops from the sleeping bag and shoving them all into his mouth. "How do you like that?" he said, spraying bits of sweet everywhere.

Madden opened his mouth to cry out, his face frozen in an expression of horror as Jack pretended to swallow his mouthful.

Peaky span around, staring at Jack in shock.

"Eurghh! These are disgusting." Jack pulled a face. "They've gone off." With his tongue, he moved the puddle of fizzing sugar into his left cheek, like a squirrel, so he could speak. "Have you got any water?" He spat onto the ground. It was turquoise.

Looking up, he tried to control every muscle in his face so that he wouldn't betray the hint of a smile as he took in the horrified expressions on Peaky's and Madden's faces. "What's the matter?"

"What did you do that for?" Madden whispered.

"Oh, I'm sorry," Jack said in a mocking tone. "Did I eat up all your yummy sweeties?"

Peaky and Madden stared at him, seemingly unable to move.

Jack put his hands over his stomach. "*Oofff*, maybe I should have put something in my empty stomach before I ate the Toxic Fizzy Drops." He swallowed a mouthful of air and brought it back up, making a terrific burping sound. "I don't feel very well."

Madden and Peaky took a step towards one another.

"What?" Jack asked innocently. "You two look like you've seen a ghost!"

"Those weren't sweets," Peaky whispered, all his bravado leaking away. He'd gone slack with shock and suddenly looked much younger.

"Oh, come on." Jack let out a nervous laugh. "I know blueberry flavoured Toxic Fizzy Drops when I see them. They *are* Toxic Fizzy Drops, aren't they?" He shifted forwards, rising up on his knees, his ankles still tied together. Peaky and Madden shuffled back, bumping against one another in their hurry to get out the door. "Urgh!" Jack grabbed his stomach. "I don't feel good." He made a retching sound and let all the sweets he'd pushed to the side of his mouth come back out. Then he collapsed on the sleeping bag with a thud. "Aaaarrrrrgghhhhhhhhh. It hurts! It hurts!" he cried, writhing around. "What's happening to me?"

Peaky and Madden were clutching each other now, watching him in horror.

Jack cried out, writhing, then shuddering, letting the turquoise foam spill out of his mouth. He tried to make his eyes roll back in his head, and blinked furiously as he kicked his legs, giving his best impersonation of a person possessed. He'd seen enough horror movies to know how to make it look good. He suddenly went still.

"Is he…" Peaky whispered, "dead?"

"He ate the rat poison!" Madden said, totally shocked.

Jack heard the boys creep towards him. He waited until their heads were right above his before he retched, rolling his eyeballs back before opening his lids and showing them the whites of his eyes. It was his favourite zombie move.

"Help me," he whispered, reaching his hand up. "I'm dying."

"Aaaarrrgghhhhhh!" Peaky and Madden yelled, jumping out of their skins.

Jack let his body flop to the ground with his eyes shut, trying not to smile as he heard the thudding sound of Peaky and Madden running away.

25

PLAYING DEAD

Jack lay still, keeping his breathing shallow. He couldn't move until he was certain Peaky and Madden had really gone. As he lay there pretending to be dead, he thought about the bearded vulture. It had arrived! He was eager to go out and see it, but he couldn't, not yet. He was comforted by the fact that, if he lifted his eyelids a fraction, he could see the outline of the air rifle through his eyelashes. It was lying discarded on the floor. The lammergeier was safe.

He was about to open his eyes and sit up when he heard something move outside. His pulse, which had only just returned to normal, sprang into a gallop. He instructed every muscle of his body to relax. Peaky and Madden must have come back for a second look, to make sure he was dead. With his mouth open a tiny crack, he tried to let air in and out of his body as quietly

223

as possible without moving his chest. He prayed they wouldn't poke him with a sharp stick.

Someone outside was creeping towards the door. He heard a gasp, and a familiar voice wailed, *"Jack?"*

Through his eyelashes Jack saw Twitch rush in and grab the box of rat poison. "NO! *Oh no!*" He fell to his knees.

Jack desperately wanted to sit up and reassure Twitch that he wasn't dead, but what if Peaky and Madden were close by, watching or listening? Nothing would convince them more of his death than someone else corroborating it.

"Jack? Jack?" Twitch shook him. "Please, Jack? Wake up!"

Jack didn't respond, though every cell in his body screamed that he should.

Twitch jumped to his feet, running out onto the heath. "Help me! Somebody! Help!" Jack could hear the distress in his voice and felt terrible. But, if Peaky and Madden hadn't been convinced that he was dead before, they would be now. He heard Twitch turn and run back. As his friend fell to the ground beside him again, Jack reached out, grabbed his wrist, and whispered, "It's all right. I'm not dead."

Twitch screamed.

Jack sat bolt upright, holding up his hands. "Shhhh. I'm OK," he hissed. "It was a trick. I didn't eat poison. I was tricking Peaky and Madden."

"*What is wrong with you?*" Twitch was shouting, the shock transforming his fear into anger. "Why would you do that?"

Jack put his finger to his lips, trying to quieten Twitch down.

Twitch snorted, jumping to his feet. "I thought you were dying!" His voice was hoarse with emotion. He was very upset. "I thought they'd made you eat rat poison!"

Jack risked poking his head out the door. He glanced around to check the coast was clear. "Please, listen to me." He took Twitch's arm and sat him down, then untied the blue rope around his ankles. "They were going to shoot the lammergeier. I didn't know what else to do. I pretended to eat the rat poison as a diversion, to frighten them. I didn't expect you to show up. It wasn't meant to scare you. I'm really sorry."

Twitch's mouth clamped shut. He blinked furiously, staring at the turquoise spittle on Jack's chin.

"It's Toxic Fizzy Drops. You know? The sweets." Jack wiped his mouth with his sleeve. "I ate Toxic Fizzy Drops. They look like rat poison."

"They were going to shoot the lammergeier?" Twitch was having a hard time piecing it all together.

Jack nodded.

"You were protecting it?"

"You have to believe me. Last night, Peaky and Madden planted dead rabbit traps and sprinkled rat poison on them to kill the vulture, but Terry had swapped out the rat poison for Toxic Fizzy Drops, so the lammergeier wouldn't be hurt."

"Terry helped you?"

"And Ava." Jack nodded. "Last night I followed Peaky and Madden, taking pictures, to get evidence so we can go to the police. They are the evil cat killers. He pulled the slingshot from his trouser pocket. They used this. The cats were target practice. Peaky wanted to shoot the vulture, but he isn't a good shot. They laid traps with poison to be sure to kill the bird. When I saw they'd brought a gun with them, I tried to sneak in and steal it, but they caught me. They were tying me up when Madden saw the vulture. Peaky was loading his gun. I didn't know what to do. I had to stop them. I saw the Toxic Fizzy Drops and put a fistful in my mouth, then gave them the best zombie death scene I could!" He paused, suddenly feeling proud. "I scared the life out of them, and they ran away, and I think, or at least I hope, they think I'm dead."

"I saw them." Twitch nodded. "I came up early, to the skywatch hide. The birdwatching website is reporting that the lammergeier is close. It might arrive today. I was looking through my binoculars when I heard shouting. I saw Peaky and Madden burst out of the shooting butt and run down the hill towards Rooky Wood. I came to see what had scared them away. I didn't expect it to be you!"

"I heard you in the doorway. I thought you were them, coming back to check if I was dead. When I realized it was you, I knew I had to let you call for help. If they'd seen you come in, and you didn't cry for help, they'd suspect a trick and come back." Jack grinned. "I'll bet they're running home as fast as they can right now." He saw the muscles in Twitch's face relax as he understood the logic of Jack's plan. "Look, Twitch, I really am sorry."

"It's all right. You were protecting the vulture."

"No, let me finish." Jack took a breath. "I've got lots of things to say sorry for and you might not want to be my friend after I've finished. I've lied to you, lots. I didn't go back to the hide on Sunday when I said I would, with Ava and Terry. We went off and investigated the case of the cat killer. We got a lead that took us to Mord Hall. Then I lied to you again about Terry having a hurt ankle. He didn't. We both went to

Mord Hall to investigate and get jobs at the party on Friday, which is why I went all weird when you started talking about trick-or-treating. I'd totally forgotten about it. I've been so caught up in the case and … well, I think I was a bit jealous of the vulture," Jack admitted. "I thought you'd want to solve a mystery with me, like we did in the summer, but as soon as you heard about the lammergeier you forgot all about the case of the cat killer. You didn't think it was important and that made me feel like I wasn't important."

"Of course I still want to be your friend! And you *are* important! It's just, the lammergeier is all I can think about." Twitch looked sheepish. "I haven't been a brilliant friend either, have I? I didn't notice the lies because I assumed you wanted to do what I wanted to do." He frowned. "Although I was confused about the ankle, because Ava said you were hurt, not Terry, but I didn't care. I only wanted to see the vulture. I thought you wanted that too."

"I do now." Jack grinned. "I just died to save that bird."

"I wish I had helped you solve the mystery. I never meant to make you feel unimportant. You're my best mate… Wait!" Twitch's eyes grew wide. "You said Madden *saw* the lammergeier…"

"It's here." Jack nodded.

The two boys scrambled to the doorway. Twitch poked his head out first. "Coast's clear," he whispered.

"Wait, put this in your rucksack. It's evidence." Jack handed Twitch the air rifle, picked up his phone, stopped the audio recording, and zipped it into his pocket for safe keeping.

Keeping low, the two boys hurried from the shooting butt.

"Follow me," Jack said, heading towards the flat rocks. If the bearded vulture was going to choose a rabbit to eat, he was certain it would be this one.

Approaching the wide rock cautiously, they saw the dead rabbit splayed on it like a primitive sacrifice. Three ravens were squabbling over it, cawing at each other as they darted in, snipping and ripping away titbits of flesh from the carcass with their beaks. Standing beside the dead rabbit with its head bowed, tearing at the meaty organs, was a bird of prey.

"That's not a lammergeier," Twitch said, pulling Jack down into the long grass. "That's a hen harrier! Madden must not know the difference."

"But he said it was massive." Jack couldn't help feeling disappointed.

"Jack, if you, Ava and Terry hadn't swapped the

poison for sweets," Twitch whispered, "all those birds would be dead." He looked at Jack with profound respect. "Thank you." He shook his head. "I don't care that you lied."

Jack felt light as a feather knowing Twitch had forgiven him. He could never stay mad at his friend for long. Twitch was Twitch. He loved birds. And Jack wouldn't be here right now if it wasn't for him. And though it wasn't a bearded vulture, it was a new bird to add to his list. Jack watched the hen harrier eat, feeling a warm burst of pride. It was worth all the kicks and the bruises and stings to have saved the lives of these birds. It wasn't big heroic work, saving a raven, or a pigeon, or a cat, but it was a small act of bravery and, he felt, an important one. He smiled, as the ravens chattered, bullying one another.

Twitch unzipped his jacket and lifted his long-lens camera over his neck. He took a picture of the hen harrier.

"A hen harrier's not a lammergeier though, is it," Jack said. "It's not our lifer."

"When you're birding, you can only hope for sightings of rare birds, you cannot expect them," Twitch whispered. "For some people being a birder is about seeing rare birds, but for me it's about seeing common birds doing uncommon things and learning about them." Silently his camera captured more pictures.

"Yeah, I know, but…" A dark shadow sailed across Jack's eyeline, blotting out the rising sun. He grabbed Twitch's arm. "Look up," he gasped, suddenly unable to breathe.

"What is it?" Twitch turned.

"Lammergeier!"

26
SPARK BIRD

The giant vulture was riding a thermal: an upward current of air created by the warmth of the sun on the ground. It turned, rising in slow circles, its wings not appearing to move. It looked as rigid and graceful as a glider.

Jack rolled onto his back, so that he was lying next to Twitch, looking up. "What's it doing?"

"It isn't interested in the meat on the rabbit. It wants the bones," Twitch replied in hushed tones. "It's waiting for the ravens and the hen harrier to pick the carcass apart."

"Look at the size of those wings!"

"At least a two-metre wingspan." Twitch pointed his camera at the bird. "It's no good. I'm only getting the silhouette."

"Should we try and get closer to the rabbit?" Jack suggested. "Before it lands?"

"We need to go quietly. We don't want to frighten away the other birds. It will send a warning signal to the lammergeier."

Jack held up his hands and signed, *"Let's use sign language."*

Twitch gave him a thumbs up.

The two boys crawled forward army-style, using their elbows, as slowly and quietly as possible.

Twitch pointed to a ditch beside the flat rock, and they slithered into it. Now, they were behind the dead rabbit with a clear view of the rock to their left. They lay in the heather-lined dip with their heads peeping through the long grass.

"Are we hidden enough?" Jack signed to Twitch, who nodded. The boys made themselves as comfortable as possible while they waited. Jack was aware of the dull ache in his muscles where Peaky and Madden had hit him, but he was more interested in the creature that looked like a feathered kite sailing overhead. He suddenly felt truly happy. He lifted his hands. *"You're the best friend I've ever had,"* he signed to Twitch, and Twitch rewarded him with a grin.

"You're the first true friend I've ever had," Twitch replied in sign. *"No one else would put up with me."*

Half an hour passed, in which they lay in

companionable silence watching the hen harrier eat its fill and disappear with a beak full of food. The ravens decimated the remains of the rabbit and then got into a fight. Lying in the heather with his best friend and a lammergeier soaring overhead was the best feeling in the world, and Jack couldn't stop smiling.

A shadow crossed their faces accompanied by the *whoomph* of wafting wings and Jack retracted his fingers into his fist, shooting a lightning-fast glance at Twitch, who grabbed Jack's hand as they witnessed the powerfully effortless landing of the lammergeier.

The bird was huge, the size of a bulldog, but utterly unlike any creature Jack had come close to in his entire life. He stopped breathing. Reality shifted. It was as if he'd pushed through an invisible film into the true world where the sky was bigger, bluer, closer. Colours were brighter. The grass was an autumn rainbow of lemon-yellow, magenta and forest-green. The earth was crawling with life: he became aware of hibernating ladybirds, scurrying woodlice and spinning spiders. The ancient rock beneath him beat a silent drum that told of millennia, and everything was slightly out of focus except the bearded vulture. The lammergeier felt impossible, an ancient creature from ages past, but it was real, and here, right now.

Jack didn't dare move.

The bird's mighty wings hung like a cloak of black and white feathers from its powerful shoulders. Jack had thought of vultures as unkempt and scruffy, with bald patches, but this lammergeier was commanding and regal. Its body and legs were clothed in ivory, the tips of the quills stained sandy-red. Its claws looked reptilian, capable of delivering a killer blow. Its ruffled neck feathers were of the deepest rust brown and its head was hawk-like, with a white forehead. Around the eye sockets was a deep black stripe that extended down past a viciously hooked beak and ended in a peculiar black beard, giving it a villainous look.

Jack had imagined the lammergeier would descend on the rabbit, ripping it apart like the ravens had, but it walked around the carcass, critically assessing the food. He stared at the bird's eyes, circled with red. Did it know that he and Twitch were lying in the grass, watching it? Could it see him? It didn't appear concerned or alarmed. The lammergeier blinked, its membranous third eyelid closing across its eyeball, and Jack shivered, thrilled and unnerved to be so close to this splendidly alien creature.

Stepping up to the rabbit in a manner that made Jack think of the powerful elderly men he'd seen entering the House of Lords, with bandy legs and red cloaks, the vulture put a claw on the torso, bobbed its head down, and took a leg bone in its beak, ripping it free. Jack was certain it was too large to eat. The vulture dropped it, then picked it up again from one end and gulped the whole thing down like a sword swallower!

Jack's mouth dropped open as the vulture did the same thing with a second bone. He glanced at Twitch, who was staring at the vulture with a similarly amazed expression. Jack had a sudden overpowering feeling that this bird should never be in a zoo or a glass case, but that it should be free to roam the earth. He could feel his idea of the world changing, growing. What other creatures were out there, sharing this planet, that he didn't know about? He wanted to find out and see them in their natural habitats.

The bearded vulture turned its head. For a moment, Jack felt the bird's powerful gaze on him. He was humbled and awestruck. He didn't mind that he'd taken a beating from Peaky and Madden for this bird. He'd take another ten for the lammergeier.

"A companion for kings!" Twitch signed to him.

Jack nodded. He'd never felt more like a king in his life.

27
LIFER

Twitch propped himself up on his elbows, poking his camera lens through the long grass to take pictures whilst the lammergeier ate. Jack was mesmerized. The vulture put a taloned claw down and pulled the tibia from what was left of the carcass. It took off and, thinking it had flown away, Jack sat up. A minute later, he was startled by a clattering, flinching as the leg bone hit the rocks, smashing to pieces. The bearded vulture landed and gobbled up the shards.

Jack felt like he could lie in the grass and watch the lammergeier for ever, but he was shivering, and Twitch had noticed. The spot they were lying in was shady and it was a cold morning. Twitch signalled that they should retreat, and as they commando-crawled backwards, away from the lammergeier's banquet of bones, Jack was increasingly feeling the aches and pains of his adventures. Twitch stopped him in a patch of sunshine, when they were far enough from the vulture to talk again. He pulled a cheese sandwich, an apple, and a flask of water from his rucksack, and insisted Jack ate all of it.

"That was amazing," Jack said, feeling better as he scoffed down the sandwiches. "The lammergeier looked right at me. Did you see? It was like… It was like…" He struggled to find the words. "It was like going back in time and staring into the face of a dinosaur! Don't you think? I didn't realize it was going to be like that. And the way it swallowed those bones whole! Whoa! Gruesome! But brilliant! I mean talk about wild! It's incredible! So real! We need to get the others. They all need to see this…" He shook his head in wonder. His heart was racing just thinking about it.

Twitch chuckled.

"What's funny?"

"The lammergeier." Twitch grinned. "I think it's your spark bird."

"My spark bird?" Jack considered this, feeling giddy. "Yeah! My spark bird!"

"Pretty cool spark," Twitch said, approvingly. "Especially seeing as you're into zombies and ghouls and stuff."

"What was your spark bird?"

"A nightjar," Twitch replied without hesitation. "One summer, when I was eight, I went camping with my grandad. We set up our tent on a bit of heathland where he said there was good birding. At dusk, I heard a strange chirruping sound; as if crickets, frogs and deathwatch beetles had formed a band and were making music. When it got dark, a bird flew up out of the bushes beside our tent. I saw its silhouette. Grandad said it was a nightjar. In the field guide I read that nightjars nest on the ground and are almost impossible to spot in daylight because they're so well camouflaged." He smiled. "That felt like a challenge.

"I spent the whole of the next day playing hide and seek with the bird. I carefully crawled around the bushes, peering in, examining every centimetre of the ground, but I couldn't see it. By the late afternoon I was certain it wasn't nesting there, and was about to give up, when something seemed to happen to my brain. I'd been sitting and staring at the same spot for so long that my vision shifted somehow, almost like it switched to a new setting, and suddenly, there it was, in focus, incredibly close to me. The nightjar was sitting in a nest, looking like a rotting log, with its eyes half closed and tiny pouting beak. It had been there the whole time, watching me, but I hadn't seen it.

"I retreated to the tent, so I wasn't threatening, and trained my binoculars on the bird. I lay on my belly watching it for hours. I saw it start making the strange calling sound, and then, at dusk, it launched itself into the sky to feast on insects. It was exhilarating. I felt like a spy that had cracked a code. After that, I don't know why, I was better at spotting birds, more interested in reading about them, and more patient when waiting for them to show themselves. The nightjar was my spark."

"And you saw a lifer today," Jack said, testing the new word. "You said the other day that the lammergeier was a lifer." He glanced at Twitch who was nodding. "So, my spark is your lifer?"

"I'll never forget today as long as I live." Twitch's expression became serious. "The lammergeier is an extraordinary bird to see, especially in this country, but, for at least sixty seconds this morning, I thought you were dead. They were the worst sixty seconds of my life." He shook his head. "Please don't do that to me again."

"I promise I won't." Jack gave him an apologetic smile, then glanced back over his shoulder to where he knew the vulture was still feeding. "But, you know, the vulture isn't safe. Lady Goremore wants it for her collection. Peaky and Madden might come back – or worse, it could be Nick Skinner. We're going to need everyone's help to protect it."

"Lady Goremore's collection?" Twitch frowned. "What collection?"

Jack realized there was so much more that Twitch still needed to know. Sitting in the sunshine he filled his friend in on all the horrors of Mord Hall and the evil cunning of Nick Skinner.

"We need to assemble the Twitchers immediately," Twitch got to his feet. "I've got Frazzle in the skywatch hide. He could take a message back to Aves Wood. Someone's bound to be there this morning."

"You brought Frazzle with you?"

"I was going to send him back to the hide with a message if I saw the bearded vulture. I tested him on Monday when you were at Mord Hall. He made it back to the hide pigeon coop no problem. That's another reason why I went back when the storm broke: to bring Frazzle home." Twitch looked at his watch. "We should go. We've been here for hours. We're trespassing and we don't want to get caught up in a hunt."

"I don't want to leave the lammergeier on Goremore land," Jack said, groaning as he stood up. His body was stiff and sore.

"Let's scare it away. Try to make it fly somewhere safe."

The two boys ran at the rock where the lammergeier was finishing up the last bits of the rabbit, hollering, whooping and clapping their hands. The vulture lifted its head, looked at them scornfully as though they were fools, before beating its powerful wings, taking to the air and rising into the clear sky. Twitch and Jack ran over the heath yelling at it, trying to drive the bird towards Passerine Pike and off the Mord Estate. Jack had no idea if it was working. The bird looked too high to hear them, and flew in circular patterns, so it seemed to be moving away but then returning.

When they reached the fence, they saw the lammergeier was circling Passerine Pike, and quickly helped each other over.

"Look." Twitch pointed and smiled. "Birdwatchers, come to see the lammergeier. It's safe whilst they have it in their sights."

The trail of people hiking up Passerine Pike had spotted the bird and were running. There were at least ten keen birders at the top already, binoculars hanging from their necks, tripods set up, all their eyes and cameras on the huge soaring bird above them.

"But this is great," Jack said, as they made their

way round to the gap in the rocks and the entrance to the skywatch hide. "Nick Skinner can't attack the vulture while all these people have their binoculars and cameras trained on it. Too many witnesses."

"So as long as the vulture carries on its journey towards the sea, and doesn't fly back to the Mord Estate, it should be safe," Twitch said. "Unless Nick Skinner is the kind of person who would chase it?"

"He is," Jack said, remembering Lady Goremore's words about the thrill of the chase. "I wonder what Peaky and Madden will do, now that they think I'm dead."

"D'you think they'll tell Nick Skinner?" Twitch said, unzipping the tent and climbing inside the skywatch hide.

"I don't know. I hope not. He's not the kind of person you want to upset. They're frightened of him and I don't blame them." Jack knew that Nick Skinner would be very angry when he found out what had happened. The longer the gamekeeper didn't know who he was, or that the lammergeier was safe, the better. "We've got Nick Skinner's gun as evidence," he said, slowly, thinking aloud, "but it won't help convict anyone of attempting to murder the lammergeier. The rabbits weren't poisoned because we stopped that. I've got audio recordings of Peaky and Madden talking, but they don't really discuss Lady Goremore or Nick Skinner. They're the guilty people behind this plot. I mean Peaky and Madden are the evil cat killers, but Lady Goremore and Nick Skinner are plotting to murder a protected bird."

"If only we could make them confess," Twitch said, pulling a silver capsule from one of the pockets of his combat trousers. He unscrewed it, took out a rolled-up piece of paper and handed it to Jack with a stub of pencil from another pocket. "What should we say?"

Jack thought for a second and then wrote: *Twitchers! Flock to the hide IMMEDIATELY. The lammergeier is here and in danger! T&J*

Twitch rerolled the paper and slipped it inside the silver canister before screwing the lid back on. Taking a ribbon of Velcro, he looped it through a slit, then he opened the square wicker basket beside him and took out Frazzle, his favourite pet pigeon.

Jack was always in awe of the way Twitch handled birds. He made it look easy, but Jack knew from experience that it wasn't. When he tried to pick up Twitch's pigeons they'd flutter away, becoming jumpy, and more than once he'd almost fallen from the viewing platform of the hide trying to grab one.

"Could you strap the message to Frazzle's leg?"

Jack attached the Velcro strap around the thin pink scaly ankle of the goggle-eyed bird. "Let's hope someone's at the hide and can get the word out."

The boys poked their heads out of the tent. The crowd of birdwatchers had grown. The Pike was surrounded. People were looking up, exclaiming excitedly and pointing.

The boys clambered out with their rucksacks on their backs, and Twitch holding Frazzle protectively against his stomach.

The lammergeier was perched proudly on the top of the Pike, looking majestic.

"What's it doing?" Jack asked Twitch anxiously. "We need it to keep flying that way."

"Vultures aren't pigeons," Twitch said, "you can't tell them where to fly. It's probably digesting breakfast." He walked away from the crowd and released Frazzle. The boys watched the pigeon arc before getting his bearings and heading towards Aves Wood.

Jack looked back at the lammergeier, then nervously swept the landscape for any sign of Nick Skinner. "It's a sitting target up there."

28

THE SPOOKTACULAR PLAN

When they reached the car park at the bottom of Passerine Pike, Jack saw Twitch's bike locked to the railing.

"You ride it," Twitch said, taking off the lock. "You're tired and hurt."

Gratefully, Jack did as he was told. He said he felt fine, but he couldn't stop shivering. He suppressed the wave of exhaustion that threatened to crash over him. He wasn't going to rest until they'd worked out how to bring Peaky and Madden to justice and had a plan to protect the lammergeier from Lady Goremore and Nick Skinner. He wanted them to be punished for what they had done to the birds in that horrible room in Mord Hall, and for attempting to murder the bearded vulture.

The floodwaters were almost drained away. There was barely five centimetres of water on the ground in town. When they reached the canal towpath, Twitch locked the bike to the railing and the boys splashed along the path to the kissing gate.

"How's the hide looking?" Jack asked, as they entered the sodden nature reserve.

"The lake has shrunk, but the hide is still a good fifteen centimetres deep in water. A lot of the soil that was shoring up the walls has been washed away. We're going to have to do some serious renovations."

Jack knew Twitch could navigate Aves Wood with his eyes closed, but he was impressed at how his resourceful friend had laid down ferns and sticks, creating a solid path across the marshiest bits of the route, so as not to drop waist-deep in water or get stuck in slurping sinking mud.

"The camouflage is gone," Jack observed with alarm when their base came into view. "People will be able to find our hide!"

"Who? We're the only people in the nature reserve," Twitch pointed out. "Everybody is at home worrying about their houses and possessions."

"Oh, Jack!" Tara called out, as the boys splashed through the water towards her. "What's happened to you? Are you OK?"

Jack turned to Twitch. "Do I look that bad?"

"Your cheek is swollen and bruised. Your lips are turquoise. You've bags under your eyes. You're covered in mud and ash, oh, and your hair's a mess."

"Mum's going to be furious." Jack sighed. "Oh, by the way, I told her—"

"You stayed at mine last night?"

"How did you guess?" Jack laughed as Twitch put an arm around his shoulders and they went into the hide together.

"I got your message from Frazzle," Tara said. "Is it true? The lammergeier's here?"

"Yes, did you tell the others?" Twitch asked.

Tara nodded. "I ran out to the bridge to get phone signal and sent a message. They're all on their way."

"Hey!"

They turned around at Terry's shout and saw him and Ozuru splashing towards the hide.

"Jack!" Terry's eyes searched his face.

"Twitch knows everything," Jack reassured him.

"Oh, phew, 'cause I couldn't hold it all in, and told Ozuru on the way here."

"I don't believe it!" Ozuru said, looking astonished. "It's true?"

"Right now, the lammergeier is perching on Passerine Pike," Twitch said, beaming.

"Is it safe?" Terry asked.

"It is for now," Twitch said. "There are loads of birdwatchers with their eyes on it. They'll log its location on the rare birds website. The big danger is if the vulture goes back onto the Mord Estate."

"I put the sweets in the box yesterday, like we planned," Terry said to Jack. "Did it work?"

"We should wait till everyone's here," Jack replied, but he was grinning and nodding.

A minute later, they heard the splashing of hurried footsteps. Ava burst into the hide, carrying Tippi on her back. "Jack!" she cried, letting Tippi drop. "Are you all right? What happened? Did they hurt you?" She put her hand up to his bruised cheek. "Did you get the evidence?" She suddenly became aware that everyone was staring at her.

Tippi made a couple of kissing sounds, but Ava shut her up with a glare.

"Let's go upstairs," Twitch said. "I need to feed Frazzle and send him home. I'm training him to nest at mine but eat at the hide, so that he knows two homes. He was starving when I let him go this morning."

"We can sit on the platform and Jack can tell us everything," Terry said.

Once all seven of them were sitting with their backs

to the tree trunk and their legs crossed or dangling over the edge, Jack outlined the case, producing the slingshot and the gun. Terry and Ava chimed in when he missed details, but Jack ended his story with a description of the evidence he'd gathered last night, and explained that Peaky and Madden thought he was dead.

Terry howled with laughter at Jack's description of his death scene. "Oh man, I'd have paid money to see it! Brilliant!"

"But the vulture's not safe," Jack said. "Lady Goremore wants it for her collection and it's sitting a stone's throw from her land."

"That woman is a monster," Tara said angrily.

"She's evil," Twitch agreed.

"You were amazingly brave last night," Ava said.

"This isn't over," Jack warned. "We need to make sure they don't get near that lammergeier ..."

"... and that they never attack any bird ever again," Terry insisted.

"... *and* that they get punished for their crimes," Ava added.

"How are we going to do that?" Ozuru asked. "Lady Goremore is powerful."

"We've got evidence," Jack said. "The pictures and the recordings."

"We're going to need more," Twitch said.

"How about…" Jack said, as an idea rose from the dead and stalked into his mind with arms outstretched, "a confession!"

"How would you get a confession from people like that?" Twitch looked doubtful.

"They are bad." Tippi nodded furiously.

"Listen," Jack said. "Tomorrow night is Halloween, right? The scariest night of the year, when the dead come to life and haunt the living…"

"What's that got to do with anything?" Terry asked. "Why are you grinning?"

"Peaky and Madden think I'm dead. If we can keep them thinking that, I might be able to frighten a confession out of them."

"But," Terry interjected, "as soon as they go to the shooting butt and find you're not there, they'll realize you're alive."

"Not necessarily."

"Dead boys tend to end up on the news," Tara pointed out.

"We only need them to believe I'm dead till tomorrow night, till the Goremore Halloween Ball." Jack's imagination was crackling with lightning. "We'll make posters, with a picture of me, saying that I'm missing, and stick them to the lampposts near Peaky's and Madden's houses."

"Won't your parents freak out?" Ozuru asked. "Mine would."

"I'll tell them it's part of a Halloween prank we're playing. They know I love Halloween."

"Me and Tippi can make the posters," Ava said. "Nan'll help us. She's got a printer on the boat."

"I'm good at posters," Tippi said enthusiastically.

"You won't be able to go home," Twitch pointed out. "You live too close to Peaky. He could see you. You can stay with me tonight, if you like."

"Thanks." Jack grinned; he loved staying over at Twitch's. "I don't suppose you've got hot water, do you? I told Mum I was going to yours for a bath last night."

They laughed as Jack held out his hands and looked down at his clothes. He was a mess.

"Ava and I will knock on Peaky's and Madden's doors and say we're part of a local search effort to find you," Terry said. "Ava can ask them if they've seen you recently, and I'll try to speak then burst into tears." The Twitchers all turned to stare at him. "What! I can make myself cry whenever I want to. It's a trick I learned when I was little, to get my big brothers into trouble."

"What if Peaky and Madden go back to the shooting butt?" Twitch said.

"I'm sure they will," Jack said. "I would. But I wouldn't go in daylight when anyone could see me. I'd wait till tonight, when it was dark." He grinned. "But we'll have got there first. Twitch, do you think Constable Greenwood would help us?"

"Probably. He's a kind man and he likes birds."

"Good, then you and I are going to pay him a visit as soon as we're done here. We'll need the help of the police if we're going to get justice for the birds and the cats."

"What about me?" Ozuru asked. "What can I do?"

"You and Tara have the most important job of all. You must go immediately to the skywatch hide and watch over the lammergeier. We need to be certain it doesn't go back to the Mord Estate. And I need you to keep an eye on the shooting butt, until we get there. If you see Peaky and Madden near it, we need to know. The plan won't work if they get there before we do."

"Got it." Ozuru nodded.

"Brilliant." Tara beamed, excited to see the vulture.

"Right," Jack clapped his hands together. "Twitch and I need to get to Constable Greenwood's house as quickly as possible."

"But what about the rest of the plan?" Tara asked.

"I'm still working it out," Jack admitted, "but it's going to be spooktacular!"

29

YELLOW TAPE

By the time they arrived at Constable Greenwood's house it was mid-afternoon. Jack had called his mum and explained that he and Twitch wanted to get ready for Halloween together. He told her to ignore the posters saying he was missing because they were doing a prank on their classmates, and he begged to stay one more night with Twitch, so they could make their costumes for trick-or-treating. Eventually she'd given in to his pleading.

"We must hurry," Jack said as Twitch rang the doorbell. "We need to get to the shooting butt and set it up before it's dark."

The door opened.

"Hello, boys," Constable Greenwood said, smiling down at them. He was in jeans, a blue jumper and grandad slippers and didn't look like a police officer at all. "What are you two doing on my doorstep? Found any more bank robbers?" He chuckled at his own joke.

"I hope we're not bothering you," Twitch said. "Only we've got something we urgently need to talk to you about. Don't we, Jack?"

Jack nodded, spying steel-toe-capped boots in the shoe rack and a police jacket with reflective strips hanging on a coat hook. "It's about a murder plot."

Constable Greenwood's eyebrows shot up. "If it's the police you're wanting, you should go to the station. I'm off-duty today."

"We don't need the police," Jack replied. "At least, not yet. We need advice about the things that are illegal and the right way to go about certain things."

Constable Greenwood blinked trying to make sense of this cryptic statement. "You'd better come in then. I was about to start making dinner, but I can give you ten minutes. I'd hate to think of you boys getting mixed up in a murder plot because I hadn't put you straight on the law."

"Don't worry," Twitch said, as they entered Constable Greenwood's cosy living room. "It's not us. We're not the ones doing something illegal." He glanced at Jack. "At least, I don't think we are."

A French bulldog was asleep on a rug beside a wood

burner. He opened his eyes and looked at them, wagged his tail a couple of times, but was too comfy to bother with a boisterous greeting.

"Well, that is a relief." Constable Greenwood indicated they should sit on his sofa. He sank into an armchair opposite. "What's this all about then?"

"The cat shootings," Jack said. "I know you're investigating them. We know who did it." He pulled the slingshot from his pocket and put it down on the coffee table. "This is the weapon that hurt those cats. It belongs to Tom Madden, but Richard Peak also used it and I heard him say he shot the cat that died."

"To report a crime, you should go to the police station," Constable Greenwood said, frowning at the weapon.

"We don't want to report the crime yet. You see, it's not the only crime they've committed, or at least, attempted to commit." Jack repeated the story of how he'd investigated the shootings, about Nick Skinner, the room upstairs in Mord Hall with the rare birds, and Lady Goremore's desire to add the lammergeier to her collection. He told the policeman how they'd foiled the attempt on the vulture's life with the sweets but that Peaky and Madden had brought a gun with them. Twitch slid the air rifle from his rucksack and put it on the table beside the slingshot. "They stole this from Nick Skinner's gun cabinet." And Jack explained how he'd tried to take the gun and had to fake his own death, but that the bird was safe, for now."

Constable Greenwood looked more and more astonished.

"I took photos of them planting the dead rabbits sprinkled with the Toxic Fizzy Drops." Jack held up his phone. "And I got a recording of them talking about doing it, and about me eating the rat poison that proves what I'm saying is true."

"Well now. That is quite a story! No, Jack, you can keep your phone. If we need those photographs, you can download them for us."

"It is illegal to try and kill the bearded vulture, isn't it, Constable Greenwood?" Twitch said.

"Yes. The Wildlife and Countryside Act of 1981 protects wild animals – including birds. An attempt to harm the bearded vulture would be a criminal offence. But we can't charge Lady Goremore or Nick Skinner on the back of a story." He looked troubled. "Tom and Richard on the other hand are going to be in a lot of trouble. Those two boys are in and out of the station, but stealing a firearm with the intention of using it on a protected animal is serious. They've no licence for a gun and, seeing as they're not yet eighteen, they're underage."

"We know you'll need evidence. That's why we came," Jack said. "There's no dead vulture, thanks to us, but who is going to believe a bunch of kids over Nick Skinner and Lady Goremore?"

"We can't let them get away with it," Twitch said, leaning forward. "They might try again, and even if they don't kill the lammergeier, they'll keep shooting protected birds."

"Where are you going with this?" Constable Greenwood frowned.

"I've thought of a way for us to get a confession out of Peaky and Madden, which will implicate Nick Skinner and Lady Goremore, giving the police a reason to search Mord Hall for the illegal birds," Jack said. "But for it to work, we're going to need your help."

"Go on," Constable Greenwood leaned forward. "I'm listening."

Jack laid out his plan, some of it only coming to him as he spoke. Constable Greenwood and Twitch listened in wide-eyed silence. "So? What do you think?"

Constable Greenwood thought for a long moment. "I cannot be seen to be part of a vigilante form of justice," he said, carefully. "However, I am going to the

Goremore Halloween Ball. A small number of tickets are made available to local officers and nurses for a reduced price. I was going to take … a friend, but considering what you've just told me, I think it would be better if I invited my colleague from the NWCU." The corner of his mouth lifted, a hint of a smile.

"What's the NWCU?" Jack asked.

"The National Wildlife Crime Unit," Twitch replied.

"You'll have to wear a costume," Jack said.

"You should go as a zombie policeman," Twitch said. "You can wear your uniform and just paint your face."

"Ha! I will do exactly that." Constable Greenwood chuckled. "Now, you understand, we can't have had this conversation. I'd get into trouble."

"Yes, sir," Jack and Twitch agreed.

"And if I knew you'd trespassed onto the Mord Estate and planned to do it again, I would have to report it, tell your parents, and reprimand you."

Jack and Twitch nodded.

"Can we leave the weapons with you?" Jack looked at the slingshot and the air rifle on the table.

"I wouldn't have let you leave with them," Constable Greenwood said, picking them up. "Now, I need to get the dinner on. I've a guest arriving in a bit and she's expecting something fancy. I'll probably be so preoccupied with my cooking, I'll forget you were ever here." He smiled. "But I must tell you, I'm impressed with your detecting and you've been incredibly brave."

"It wasn't me," Twitch said. "It was all Jack." He looked proudly at him.

"Well, as an adult I also need to tell you, Jack, that you've been reckless and foolish, and you've broken the law." Constable Greenwood's voice was light, but his expression serious. "Now, on your way out, under no circumstances, must you *look in that drawer.*" He nodded towards the bottom drawer of a set below the coat hooks and winked. "You'd better get going. You've work to do."

The boys stood up.

"I'll see you at the Halloween Ball tomorrow night," he said, getting up and taking the slingshot and air rifle with him into the kitchen.

Twitch looked at Jack, then both boys looked at the drawer.

When Jack pulled it open, he saw it contained reels of yellow "crime scene" tape. He grinned, grabbed two – handing one to Twitch – then they let themselves out.

"Climb on the back," Twitch said, getting on his bike and putting his foot on the pedal.

"We need to stop off at the pound shop on the way to the shooting butt," Jack said, hopping on. "We need bin bags and a can of spray snow."

It was dusk when Jack and Twitch arrived at the skywatch hide, breathless from running up Passerine Pike. Jack was bone tired, but time was running out. He had to keep going and get to the shooting butt before Peaky and Madden, or his plan would be ruined.

All of the Twitchers were there, waiting. Nan and Tara's dad were standing with the other birders, gazing at a circling silhouette on the horizon. They'd spent the afternoon watching the vulture, who'd perched on the Pike for a while then ridden a thermal up into the sky.

"Has it gone?" Jack asked hopefully.

"Unlikely. It's late. It needs to find somewhere to roost for the night," Twitch said.

"I wish we could make it fly away."

"Peaky was at Madden's house," Ava reported. "They looked terrified. Terry's crying was amazing. He said he was your best friend, Jack. They looked so guilty when he burst into tears. They couldn't shut the door fast enough."

"We've had our binoculars trained on the shooting

butt the whole afternoon," Ozuru reported. "No one's been near it."

"Let's hope Peaky and Madden were too cowardly to tell Nick Skinner what happened," Jack said. "He'll think the vulture's been eating poison."

"We've been watching the lammergeier all afternoon," Tara said, her joyful eyes dancing. "It's a powerfully beautiful bird. I thought my father was going to cry when he first saw it."

"You saved it," Twitch reminded Jack and everyone nodded.

"It's not safe yet," Jack said, feeling buoyed up on the wave of admiration from his friends. "This isn't over until we catch the plotters and make sure they can never hurt a bird again."

"Right," Twitch agreed. "Let's get going. We need to work quickly."

"I'll stay here with Tippi," Ava said. "We'll keep the grown-ups distracted and looking the other way, won't we, Tippi?"

"I should stay too," Tara said, glancing at her father. "My dad will notice if I disappear. He won't like it."

Terry, Ozuru, Twitch and Jack ran to the fence and waited till they heard Tippi shouting, "Look at me! I can do cartwheels!" Then they helped each other over and sprinted to the shooting butt, keeping low, following Jack.

It was exactly as Jack and Twitch had left it that morning.

Twitch took a roll of bin bags from his rucksack. "Put all of their stuff into these bags."

Ozuru and Terry sprang into action.

"I think I died about here," Jack said, lying down on the ground.

Twitch went over and stood in the doorway. "No, a little bit more to your right, and put your feet together. Your ankles were tied, remember? That's better. Turn your head. That's it. That's how I saw you this morning. I'll never be able to get that image out of my head." He took out the can of fake snow and followed the line of Jack's body, spraying a white outline on the ground. When he was finished, Jack sprang up. "Nice!" He grinned.

"We've got everything," Terry said.

"Take out the bags," Jack instructed, pulling out a reel of the yellow tape with *CRIME SCENE DO NOT CROSS* printed on it. He peeled back the end and followed the others outside. "Here, hold this." Jack passed Twitch the end of the yellow tape and walked around the shooting butt several times. He did a criss-cross of yellow tape across the doorway for good measure, then stood back to admire their handiwork. The white outline of Jack's body on the floor was clearly visible through the doorway and the crossed tape.

"If that doesn't persuade them that they're in big trouble, nothing will," he said with grim satisfaction. "Right, let's get out of here."

30

HALLOWEEN BALL

"I hope this works," Terry said nervously, as he, Jack and Twitch approached the open kitchen door of Mord Hall.

The three boys were smartly dressed in white shirts and black trousers, the uniform of the hired kitchen hands for the Halloween Ball – and luckily, also their school uniform.

"It'll work," Jack said under his breath, his heart racing. "It has to."

Ken Mulworthy looked up as they paused on the doorstep. Jack saluted. "Here we are, sir, reporting for duty." He gave the man his most winning smile.

"Great," Ken replied. "I thought there were only two of you."

"Mrs Mulworthy said I could bring a friend." Jack pointed at Twitch. "This is Corvus."

Twitch shuffled through a series of expressions, trying to look employable.

"Well, there's no shortage of work. Welcome, Corvus," Ken replied. "Right, follow me, you three. I'll show you where the sinks are."

Relieved, Jack glanced at Terry and Twitch. They were over the first hurdle. Hurrying to fall in step beside Ken, Jack said, "I've got a bag with our going-home clothes. Is there somewhere I can put it?"

"You can leave it in the boot room," Ken said, taking them through the main kitchen and out to a smaller room beyond.

"Mr Mulworthy," Jack said, amiably. "Do you know Richard Peak? He's working tonight and lives across from me. My mum was hoping I might be able to get a lift home with him afterwards."

"Yes, I know Richard." Ken sighed. "He's our gamekeeper's nephew. He and his friend Tom are waiting on the top table tonight." He shook his head. "I don't know whose idea that was, although I could hazard a guess. That pair should be schooled in manners before being allowed to wait on lords and ladies." He pointed to a wall with two sinks. "The crockery will need to be washed by hand. There are two dishwashers for the glasses. During the party I want you to go around collecting the empties and any discarded dishes you see and bring them in here. Stack the machines with the glasses and turn them on. The cycle is twenty minutes. When the glasses are clean, they'll need drying and taking back to the bar in the library. Got that?"

They all nodded.

"Under no circumstances are any of you allowed to drink anything other than the refreshments Mum, Mrs Mulworthy, will provide. If you drink anything from the glasses, you'll be sent home with no pay. Understand?"

They all nodded again.

"Good. That's the door to the boot room where you can put your stuff." He paused for Jack to stash his rucksack inside. "Now, there's cleaning to be done before the party set up. All the glass display cabinets in the grand hall need polishing. After that I'm going to need help setting up the tables and chairs in the banqueting hall."

The boys bobbed their heads.

"Let's get the cleaning done first." Ken pointed at two buckets full of cloths and spray-gun cleaners. "Grab those and follow me. There are lots of people getting this place shipshape for tonight, and I'm in charge of all of them," he said, as they walked through the house.

"I'm going to leave you to get on with it. There's the entrance hall, I'll be in the library if you need me."

"How did you know Peaky and Madden were working at the party tonight?" Terry asked Jack in a low voice.

"I overheard them talking about it," Jack replied under his breath. "They were sad that they wouldn't be able to steal little children's trick-or-treat sweets."

Terry rolled his eyes. "They are literally the dictionary definition of a bully!"

"Yeah, well, they're about to experience a Halloween trick that they'll never forget." Jack smiled, darkly.

As they came into the grand entrance hall, Jack glanced worriedly at Twitch.

His friend took in the display cases of stuffed songbirds. "This place is ghastly."

"It doesn't need Halloween decorations," Jack agreed, picking up a spray-gun of window cleaner and a cloth from the bucket. "It's spooky enough already."

As he polished one of the cases, Jack stared at the glassy-eyed stuffed birds glued to their twigs and remembered how vividly alive the eyes of the lammergeier were. He thought about the regal vulture. It had spent last night on Passerine Pike, so Ozuru and Terry had camped out in the Skywatch hide to guard it. Much to Jack's dismay, the vulture had then hung around the Pike all morning. Ozuru had finally got to employ his rota and the others were taking shifts, in pairs, to watch the bird. He and Tara were there right now. Jack hoped that, with Peaky and Madden working, and Nick Skinner and Lady Goremore going to the party, the bearded vulture would be safe tonight.

He thought about the dreadful room at the top of the sweeping stairs, with the pedestal and the empty case, and he polished the glass in front of him with an angry vigour. Looking over, he saw Twitch working with the same focused fury.

The boys were busy cleaning for several hours. As they moved around Mord Hall, they noted useful doorways, windows and anything that would help them pull off Jack's master plan.

At five o'clock more workers arrived. The house buzzed with industrious people. A team poured out of a van, adorning Mord Hall with pumpkin lanterns, skulls, cobwebs and other spooky decorations. Three men set up a bar in the library. A person they called "the shucker" arrived with a barrel of oysters, and a troop of waiters and waitresses filed into the banqueting hall dressed in black shirts and black trousers with pulled-back hair.

"Hide," Twitch gasped, pushing Jack. "Peaky and Madden are here!"

Jack ducked behind Terry and Twitch, as a subdued Richard Peak and Tom Madden traipsed past with the other waiting staff.

"Well, at least we know they're not out looking for the lammergeier," Twitch whispered.

"I should go back to the kitchen," Jack said. "They mustn't see me."

"Look" – Terry pointed – "out there in the lobby. It's Vernon and Clem."

"What're they doing here?" Twitch looked worried. "They'll know you're not dead. If they talk to Peaky or Madden, they could ruin everything."

"Or, they could be helpful," Jack said, peeping out to check the banqueting hall doors were closed. "They know about our investigation into the cat shootings. Vernon was one of our suspects. Wait here and let me know if Peaky or Madden come out of that door." He dashed over to their classmates. "Hey, we're working at the party too." He pointed to Terry and Twitch. "Thanks for the tip off."

Vernon nodded at Terry and Twitch.

"We're on cloakroom duty," Clem said. "We have to take the guests' coats, hang them up and hand out a raffle ticket."

"Listen" – Jack lowered his voice – "d'you remember back in the summer when you rescued me from that bank robber?"

"That was awesome." Clem and Vernon nodded enthusiastically.

"Well, tonight" – Jack's voice became a whisper – "something similar's going to go down at this party." He gave them a conspiratorial wink. "Want to help? It's gonna be deadly."

"You bet." Vernon nodded enthusiastically. "Will there be fighting?"

"Maybe," Jack replied.

"Cool!" Vernon punched his fist into his open hand.

"What do you want us to do?" Clem asked.

"Nothing for now. Act normal. But before the party starts, I'm going to bring Tara and Pamela in, dressed like us. Can they join you in the cloakroom? We need to pretend they're working."

"Pammy's coming?" Clem flushed pink. "Cool. Yeah. Whatever. If you want. We don't mind. No problem."

"They know the plan. They'll tell you what we're going to do."

"Got it," Clem replied. "You can count on us."

"Oh, and don't breathe a word about this to anyone." Jack put his finger to his lips.

Vernon gave Twitch and Terry a thumbs up.

"What did you say to them?" Twitch asked when Jack returned.

"They're going to help us."

"We should get back to the washing-up room before you're seen." Twitch checked his watch. "We've got fifteen minutes before we have to meet Ozuru, Tara, Pamela, Ava and Tippi by the stable."

"I still don't understand why you're letting Pamela help," Terry grumbled as they hurried back, keeping an eye out for Peaky or Madden.

"She has a right to avenge Splatty, and besides," Jack replied, "she was great when we caught the bank robber."

"A fact she never lets us forget." Terry rolled his eyes.

Once they were back in the washing-up room, Jack pulled his coat on. "I'll tap on the kitchen window when I've got the others. Tap back if the coast is clear and we'll rush through to the boot room."

Sneaking out the back door, Jack found darkness was descending. The exterior lights were on. They had the effect of solidifying the mist in the yard. Perfect Halloween weather. He shivered, anticipating what was to come. "Please let it work," he whispered, as he hurried across the cobbles to the stables.

"Pssstttt!" he hissed. "It's me."

Ava's eyes and nose appeared over a stable door. "Hi."

A second later four more heads appeared: Ozuru, Tara, Pamela and Tippi.

"What's Tippi doing here?" Jack asked.

"We told Nan we were going trick-or-treating. I couldn't very well leave her behind."

"I'm a Twitcher too," Tippi said, sounding hurt. "I want to help catch the bird killers."

"You are." Jack smiled apologetically at her. "I shouldn't have said that. Sorry."

"That's all right." Tippi beamed.

"How's the vulture?" Jack asked Ozuru and Tara.

"Still roosting on top of the Pike," Tara replied.

"We think it's there for the night now," Ozuru added.

"OK, good, well Peaky and Madden are here, so I think it's safe for now." He did a quick check to make sure no one was watching. "I'm going to take you through the kitchen, into the sink-room, where we're doing the washing up. Past it is a boot room. Ava, Tippi and Ozuru, you'll hide in there. Terry's going to take Pamela and Tara to the cloakroom. Clem and Vernon are in charge of it."

"What fool gave those two a job?" Pamela said.

"A helpful one, because they've agreed to let you pretend you were hired to help run the cloakroom too," Jack replied. "You guys need to keep an eye on Peaky and Madden. We must know where they are at all times."

"Oh, I'll watch them all right," Pamela said, her voice flinty. She knew they were the ones who'd hurt Splatty.

"Ozuru will take over from me in the washing-up room, joining Twitch and Terry on the stage management team."

"And us?" Ava put her hand on Tippi's shoulder.

"You're in charge of costume and make-up." Jack grinned. "Now. Everyone, follow me."

31
MONSTER MASH

The boot room had a slate floor, low wooden shelves stacked with wellingtons and walking boots, and high shelves displaying riding crops and helmets. There was a thin wardrobe, in which hung a handful of wax jackets, which was where Jack had put his rucksack. Tara and Pamela took off their coats and hung them up before following Terry out of the kitchen.

Jack pulled out his rucksack and handed it to Ava. "Everything is in there."

Opening it, Ava pulled out a carrier bag and recoiled. "Ew, it stinks!"

"That's authentic mud, blood and sweat that is," Jack said, sitting down on the low shelf and pulling his smart shoes off. "The smell is part of the costume."

In a few short minutes, Jack was dressed in the exact muddy, ash-smeared clothes he'd been wearing when Peaky and Madden had seen him die.

Tippi pulled a werewolf mask and a washbag out of the front pocket of the bag and laid out the make-up on the bench beside Jack. She grinned up at her sister, and the pair of them got to work painting his face.

When they were done, Jack checked his watch. It was ten to seven; guests would start arriving any minute. He stuffed the rubber werewolf mask, which covered his whole head, into his coat pocket.

"Let's see," Terry said, poking his head around the door.

Jack got up and held his arms outstretched.

"Wow! You look really terrible." Ozuru chuckled.

"Dead-ly," Twitch agreed.

"I did his purple eyes and white face," Tippi said. "Ava put the mud in his hair."

"And the fake blood," Ava added.

"I got the contact lenses last Halloween." Jack was particularly proud of the milky pupils ringed with bloodshot veins. "They really make me look dead."

"You certainly smell like you're dead," Ava said, pulling a face.

"Here's the mixture of blueberry toxic fizz and sherbet." Twitch handed Jack a small brown envelope. "We've all got one."

"It works best if you mix it with cola in your mouth," Ozuru said as Jack slipped it into his other pocket.

"Shall we go and watch the guests arrive?" Jack asked Twitch. He felt a thrill of excitement, peppered with fear.

The two boys dashed through the haze of fine rain, running around the outside of the house, stopping at the corner and creeping through the flower bed to watch the cars rolling up the drive of Mord Hall. The front door was wide open. Red light spilled down the steps. At the bottom stood two footmen, each with large umbrellas. A smoke machine exhaled white plumes along the ground, hiding their feet and giving the impression they were hovering, as they helped guests from their vehicles and escorted them up the steps. A gaggle of paparazzi with cameras took pictures of the guests as they were greeted by Jones, the butler, who presented them with a bubbling green drink from his circular silver tray.

"We could use that smoke machine," Jack said.

"Tara might be able to grab it, once the guests have all arrived."

The great and the good from Briddvale and beyond arrived in their Halloween finery. A string quartet in the grand entrance hall played music to greet them. A skeleton arrived, escorting a woman in a towering blonde wig dressed as Marie Antoinette. One gentleman was wearing a purple velvet suit, carrying a prosthetic model of his own head under one arm and a sword in the other. Dracula and Poison Ivy mounted the steps, sheltering under an umbrella. The Wicked Witch of the West, Cruella de Vil and Frankenstein's creature all came to the ball. Jack ducked as a zombie movie star got out of a familiar red car and was joined by her zombie husband wearing aviator sunglasses. It was his mum and dad. Jack's nerves fizzed. There were a lot of people at this party that he had to avoid.

"Look, it's Constable Greenwood," Twitch whispered as a police car pulled up and parked. From it climbed two zombie police officers. "Jack, I think you might single-handedly be responsible for all the zombies here tonight." Twitch grinned.

"We should go back," Jack said, suddenly feeling overwhelmed by what they were about to do.

"Wait." Twitch held up his hand. "Is that Nick Skinner?"

Both boys watched as the bandy-legged, stocky man in a flat cap and wax jacket came out of Mord Hall, followed by a sheepish looking Peaky and Madden. He led them down the steps, away from the guests, to the flower bed where Twitch and Jack were hiding.

"Why haven't I heard from you?" Nick Skinner was growling.

Jack grabbed his phone and clicked on the audio recorder.

"We laid the traps, like you said," Peaky whined.

"Then why is the bird alive and sitting on Passerine Pike?" Nick spat. "If you'd done your job properly, it'd be lying dead somewhere."

"We did exactly as you told us," Madden echoed. "We laid four traps and put the poison in the rabbits, just like you wanted."

"I thought you were going to bring the bird to me."

"We couldn't stay out on the moor." Peaky's voice was quivering.

"Why not?"

"There was this boy," Madden said.

"Shhh." Peaky shook his head.

"What boy?"

"We were only going to rough him up a bit," Madden said, ignoring Peaky.

"What happened?"

"He ate the rat poison," Madden admitted. "He thought it was sweets."

Peaky made a weird high-pitch noise, his eyes wide with fear as he looked at his uncle. "I don't want to go to prison, Uncle Nick."

Nick Skinner's face was as unreadable as stone. "Are you telling me there's a dead boy up there, but the bird is alive?"

Peaky and Madden nodded.

Nick Skinner turned away.

"Where are you going, Uncle Nick?"

"To get a spade and a shotgun."

"Why?" Madden asked.

"Bury the boy. Shoot the bird." He shook his head as he strode away, muttering, "If you want something doing..."

Twitch's head snapped round to look at Jack in alarm.

Jack indicated they should creep away.

"That wasn't so bad," they heard Peaky saying brightly. "I thought he'd be angrier than that."

"He will be," Madden muttered, "when he gets up there and sees that the body's gone and the police have been snooping around."

Jack couldn't even feel a glimmer of satisfaction that his ruse had worked. He was too frightened for the vulture. He and Twitch slowly moved back the way they had come. Once Peaky and Madden were out of sight, they pelted towards the courtyard.

"Jack, can you manage without me?" Twitch said.

"What're you going to do?"

"I've got my bike. I can get up to Passerine Pike before Nick Skinner. There are birdwatchers camping up there. They'll help me protect the lammergeier if I tell them what's happening."

"I'll come with you," Jack said. "Nick Skinner is dangerous."

"No, we need evidence that Lady Goremore is behind all this. You must carry on with your plan. Ozuru and Ava can help me. We've got our phones. We'll message you if anything happens."

"Constable Greenwood is here," Jack said. "I'll ask him to send a police car up to the car park."

"Yes. Do that." Twitch bolted through the kitchen door and ran out two minutes later with Ozuru and Ava. The three of them sprinted across the yard to the stables where they'd parked their bikes.

"Guess it's just us," Terry said, coming out of the back door and standing with him in the yard.

"Yeah." Jack felt shaken. He tried to gather his thoughts.

Tara came to the door with Tippi. "The last guests

have arrived. I managed to get the smoke machine and stuff it into a pumpkin. It's plugged-in underneath the big dresser in the banqueting hall. Pamela put the Bluetooth speaker under the top table." She paused. "What's the matter? Where are the others?"

"Nick Skinner's gone to hunt the vulture." Jack heard Vernon's words in his head: *"If Nick Skinner shoots at something, it dies. He never misses."* "Twitch, Ozuru and Ava have gone to protect it." He tried to smile. "It's up to us to get that confession."

"Ken said the gong for dinner will be struck at eight. That's the sign for everyone to go to the banqueting hall." Terry looked nervous. "After everyone's sat down, Lady Goremore will give a toast. Then the waiters deliver the first course. It's pumpkin and truffle soup."

"That's when I'll do it," Jack said. He looked at Tara. "Can you make sure there's a good amount of smoke in the room, to cover me?" He was conscious of his heartbeat pulsing in his neck.

"It's almost twenty to eight now," Terry said.

"Then I should go round the front and make my way into position." Jack took the werewolf mask out of his pocket and pulled it on. He was glad it hid his face. He was struggling to breathe calmly, and he didn't want the others to know that he was scared.

"Vernon is expecting you," Tara said. "Pamela's taken Clem around to the French doors at the end of the banqueting hall. She said she has her own plan." Tara shrugged. It was impossible to get Pamela to do anything she didn't want to.

"At least Nick Skinner's not in the room any more," Terry said, and Jack did find some comfort in this fact. He'd been genuinely frightened of being attacked by the man, but now he was worried the gamekeeper would attack the lammergeier, or his friends.

"Good luck, everyone," Jack said, giving them a thumbs up, before marching back round to the front of the house. The doors were closed now that all the guests were inside.

Vernon let Jack in the cloakroom window. From there he slunk into the crowd of people sipping their bubbling drinks in the entrance hall. He made a beeline for the library. His werewolf mask meant that not one person looked at him as if he shouldn't be there.

He stiffened as everyone started to applaud.

Lady Goremore was standing at the top of the sweeping staircase in the grand hall, frozen like a statue, striking a pose. She was wearing a shimmering gold dress heavily fringed with feathers and covered with a corset of sculpted bones. Her feathered headdress met in a beak-like point above her forehead; from it dripped blood-red crystals.

Bile rose in Jack's gut. She was dressed as a bird of prey. All he could think was that the feathers she wore were once on living birds, flying free.

The string quartet played an eerie waltz, as Lady Goremore descended the stairs in time to the music, her undulating arms setting the feathered sleeves fluttering.

Jack's insides flared with anger. Why were people clapping this cruel woman for wearing a dress with parts of a dead bird's body hanging from it? If they knew what she had upstairs in that room, they would not be applauding her.

He pushed his way through the gawping admirers, glad of the werewolf mask. In the library, beyond the bar, was a door behind a curtain that he'd found earlier with Terry. On the other side of it was a dead space and another door, which opened into the banqueting hall.

Jack stood beside the curtain, surreptitiously reaching behind it to turn the handle of the door. Scanning the room to make sure everyone's eyes were on Lady Goremore, he opened the door and disappeared inside.

Standing in the darkness, a calm determination overcame the nerves that had been making his chest tight. It was time to fight back. It was showtime and Jack intended to give the performance of his life.

He jumped as the dinner gong sounded.

"This is it," Jack whispered to himself through gritted teeth. "Time to terrify the truth out of them."

32

THRILLER

Through the closed door, Jack could hear the growing chatter of guests entering the banqueting hall and finding their tables.

"Don't the candles and the smoke make it marvellously spooky in here?" he heard one guest say. "It's like dining in Dracula's mansion."

"I heard the Goremores have a family tomb under the house. Perhaps they'll be joining us for dinner."

"I'm looking forward to the food. Last year the starter was a tiny roast quail served with pancetta. Delicious."

Chairs scraped and feet scuffled as people moved around their tables looking for their place names. Thin tendrils of smoke coiled up under the door, winding around his feet. He hoped the smoke was going to be thick enough to hide him.

Jack had memorized the table seating plan. The top table, where Lady Goremore and her husband would be, was facing the round tables where all the other guests would sit.

The sound of people moving died down and relaxed chatter grew louder. Everyone must be seated. Lady Goremore's toast would be coming soon.

Taking the small can of cola Ozuru had given him from his coat pocket, Jack cracked it open. He popped a capsule into his mouth, squirrelling it away between his back teeth and his cheek.

He risked opening the door into the banqueting hall a chink and putting his eye to it.

He could clearly see the top table. Lady Goremore was sitting in a giant wooden throne next to an older man with a moustache. Jack guessed this was Lord Goremore. He picked out the route he would take to the top table.

Lady Goremore lifted her hands and the room immediately fell quiet, as if the guests were under her spell. She rose to her feet, a crystal glass of the green bubbling drink in one hand.

It's now or never, Jack thought. Dropping to his knees, he crawled out into the smoke.

He heard the chime of teaspoon against crystal as he scuttled between the tables. Under the cover of the smoke, he crept along the floor, unnoticed by the mesmerized guests who only had eyes for Lady Goremore.

"Welcome to the annual Mord Hall Halloween Ball," Lady Goremore said. "We're here to celebrate Halloween in style and raise money to help unfortunate children." She paused for applause and the accompanying swell of agreeable murmuring. "And of course, I'd like to wish my darling Humbolt a happy birthday." She put her hand on his shoulder and smiled coldy down at him.

"I love a good party," Humbolt said, his curled moustache twitching comically above his daft smile, and everyone laughed.

As Jack approached the top table, the smoke got thicker and he sent up a prayer of thanks to Tara.

"I ask you all to raise your glasses." Lady Goremore held up hers. "And join me in a Halloween toast: *As vengeful ghosts roam the land, let's dance till dawn and indulge our heart's darkest desires*." She lifted the glass to her lips and took a sip.

"... *dance till dawn and indulge our heart's darkest desires*!" everyone in the hall echoed. The sound of chinking glasses gave Jack the cover he needed to slide right up to the corner of the top table and slip under the tablecloth unseen.

Moving silently, Jack crawled to the middle of the table, facing the knees of Lord and Lady Goremore, with his back against the crisp linen cloth. Lady Goremore's toast had made him angry. He knew what her darkest desires were. They were murderous, and he didn't think they should be indulged in the slightest.

Worrying about Twitch and the others, he slid his phone out of his pocket. There were no messages. He took out the brown envelope, poured the sherbet and blueberry Toxic Fizzy Drops mix into his mouth with a dribble of cola from the small can. He had to push his lips together because of the immediate powerful fizzy eruption.

The enormous pair of wooden doors into the banquet hall were pulled open. Hearing them, Jack lifted the cloth and saw a shoal of waiters and waitresses pour into the room, each carrying a steaming hot bowl of soup.

Two pairs of feet approached the top table from behind Lord and Lady Goremore. He leaned forward and peeped up, seeing Peaky and Madden, both concentrating on not spilling their bowls of soup.

The room filled with chatter as guests turned to look over their shoulders at the food that was being brought to them.

This is it!

As Peaky and Madden's feet got closer and closer to the table, Jack pushed himself backwards, sliding out the other side. He watched as Lord and Lady Goremore turned to look at the food coming towards them and then he rose to his feet in a swirl of smoke. Standing unnaturally still, he stared at Peaky and Madden through his milky contact lenses.

Peaky saw Jack first and froze in open-mouthed horror. Jack tucked his chin, opened his lips and let the rabid turquoise froth spill out. Then he bit down on the fake blood capsule he'd been holding at the back of his mouth and gave him a truly gruesome smile.

Peaky let out a blood-curdling scream, hurling his bowl of soup forwards, as if to ward Jack off, flinging it into Lady Goremore's face. She cried out in shock.

An alarmed Madden followed Peaky's gaze, gasping when he saw Jack and letting go of his bowl in fright. It smashed on the ground, splattering soup everywhere.

Jack dropped back down into the smoke and vanished.

33

TRICK OR TREAT

"What the hell do you think you're playing at?" Lady Goremore barked at Peaky, wiping soup from her face with her napkin.

But Peaky wasn't listening to her. He was looking at Madden. "It was him!" he whispered, pointing to the empty space before the table. "He was there. I saw him."

"I saw him too!" Madden mumbled, nodding.

"A ghost!" Peaky wailed. "It was a ghost."

"My dress is ruined!" Lady Goremore cursed as she looked down at her pumpkin splattered skirt. Her face twisted in rage. *You idiots! Have you any idea how much this dress cost?*

The banqueting hall had gone deathly quiet as everyone watched the drama unfolding at the top table. Hidden beneath a neighbouring table, Jack grinned; his plan was working. He took out his phone and pressed play on one of the audio files Ozuru had helped him prepare.

"*Is he … dead?*" Peaky's shocked voice came from the speaker Pamela had planted beneath the top table. It was loud.

"*He ate the rat poison!*" Madden's voice said a moment later.

"I didn't say that!" Madden shouted in a panic. "That wasn't me!"

"No, no, no!" Peaky murmured, shaking his head vigorously, his eyes wide. "No, no, no!"

"What is going on?" Lady Goremore demanded, standing up and opening the question out to the rest of the room as she looked around accusingly.

"It's not us, your ladyship." Peaky was snivelling. "It's the dead boy. We're being haunted."

"We didn't kill him. He killed himself," Madden shouted. "It was an accident. He ate the poison all by himself."

"What are you talking about?" Lady Goremore scowled at them.

"We don't want to go to prison." Peaky was pleading.

Jack hit play on the second audio file.

"*Should we put a rabbit out here, to encourage the vulture bird this way?*"

"How many do we have in the bag?"

"Four."

"We need one for the rocks by Passerine Pike, one for the track that leads up to it…"

"If we put one here the bag will be lighter."

"If we put one here, and people who aren't from the Mord Estate find it, we could be in big trouble."

"Then let's dump one on the other side of the fence."

"Uncle Nick said it's got to be where there are no trees, so the vulture can see it."

"You carry the sack then. They stink. You can put on the rat poison too. It's gross."

"If I'm doing the baiting then you can carry the bag. Or else why are you here?"

Peaky and Madden came together, clutching one other, moving away from Lady Goremore as they looked around for the invisible source of their own voices.

The room had suddenly become a theatre and the top table a stage upon which a dark scene was playing out; the ball guests couldn't work out if what they were seeing was real or a performance, but Jack heard angry murmurs at the recording.

Jack dived back through the smoke, under the top table, in between Lord and Lady Goremore's chairs, and out the other side. He rose up behind Lady Goremore, letting his head loll to one side, opened his mouth and pulled his best zombie face.

Lady Goremore, who'd clearly understood what the recorded conversation was about, and wanted it silenced, shouted, "Get those idiots out of here!" She leaned forward, suddenly exposing Jack, blood dripping from his blue and frothing mouth.

Jack raised a finger and pointed at the horrified Peaky and Madden.

Screaming, Peaky and Madden turned to run out the enormous wooden doors. But Terry, Tara and Tippi had closed them. They were standing in front of them, barring their way. As Peaky and Madden approached, the three Twitchers opened their mouths into wide alarming smiles, letting blueberry foam fizz trickle out.

"*Aaarrghhhh!*" Peaky and Madden pivoted, running the other way.

"It's not real. He's not there. It's not real. He's not there," Peaky was chanting as he clattered clumsily between the round tables, bumping into chairs.

"It was your idea to kill that vulture," Madden shouted, pushing Peaky from behind. "This is your fault."

"It wasn't my idea!" Peaky howled. "It was Uncle Nick!"

"Richard, Thomas, are you all right?" came the calm, kind voice of Constable Greenwood. "Do you need my help?"

"We didn't mean it to happen," Peaky blubbered as he stumbled towards the policeman. "He ate the poison. He thought it was sweets."

"What poison?"

"Rat poison. Richie's uncle Nick gave it to him to kill the vulture," Madden explained.

"When was this?"

"Yesterday morning." Peaky was really crying now, big snotty gulping sobs. Jack almost felt sorry for him.

"And where was this?"

"The shooting butt up by Passerine Pike."

"I think it would be a good idea if we took a trip to the station, and you tell us exactly what happened up by Passerine Pike yesterday morning, don't you?" Peaky and Madden were nodding. "And where is your uncle now, Richard? I think we should talk to him about this too."

"You can't." Peaky sniffed, wiping his nose on his sleeve. "He's gone to shoot the vulture."

"Has he now?" Constable Greenwood turned to Lady Goremore. "Lord and Lady Goremore, were either of you aware that your gamekeeper is attempting to shoot a protected bird on or close to your land?"

"I beg your pardon!" Lady Goremore balked at the question. "How dare you!"

"I'm afraid, we will have to ask you to come to the station and give a statement," Constable Greenwood said. "Although, you may want to change first."

There was a ripple of stunned laughter.

"Richard Peak and Thomas Madden, I'm arresting you for the crime of attempting to kill a lammergeier," said a strong female voice, "a protected wild animal on the red list."

"And exactly who do you think you are?" Lady Goremore was glaring at the woman standing beside Constable Greenwood.

"I'm Wildlife Crime Officer French, from the NWCU. I believe you already know Constable Greenwood from the Briddvale Police Force."

"Now hang on just a minute!" Lady Goremore barked, pumpkin soup dripping down her front. "This is *my* house, and *my* land, and you are spoiling *my* party!" She raised her hand. "GET OUT!"

A camera flashed.

"Don't you take pictures of me!" Lady Goremore wheeled around.

Jack climbed up onto the tabletop. "Wildlife Crime Officer French, I would like to report another crime.

Upstairs, Lady Goremore has a private taxidermy collection of birds of prey. She's obsessed with them. You'll find a white-tailed eagle, a peregrine falcon, merlin, goshawk, honey buzzard, red kite and loads more."

"LIES!" Lady Goremore screeched at him. "ALL LIES!"

"Oh yeah?" Jack clapped back. "What dead thing did you come to this party dressed as?"

Lady Goremore floundered, unable to respond.

"Trick or Treat, Lady Goremore," Jack said. "Trick or Treat!"

34
SOMEBODY'S WATCHING ME

"And there you have it, my fellow YouTubers!" Pamela sprang up from a table halfway down the room. Clem stood up too, turning on a ring light as he walked backwards aiming a phone at her. "The Twitchers have solved the crime of the century!" Pamela declared, talking into a handheld microphone like a TV news journalist. "Who shot Splatty, my darling fluffy puss cat?" She pointed to Peaky and Madden, announcing dramatically, "There are the evil cat killers who have been terrorizing Briddvale."

The party guests turned from Lady Goremore to look at Peaky and Madden, muttering with bewildered dismay.

"Whilst investigating Splatty's shooting, the Twitchers uncovered a dastardly plot to murder a rare bird! A weird vulture with a beard!" She raised her finger. "But that's not the worst of their crimes. You all heard Jack accuse Lady Goremore of illegally collecting dead birds of prey, well, your roving reporter, Pamela Hardacre, is about to take you upstairs for an exclusive sneak peek at Lady Goremore's private museum of murdered birds! I've been told there's an empty case up there, waiting for the poor bearded vulture! Let's go see her creepy bird tomb, shall we?" She stopped talking and smiled prettily at the phone.

Jack had never liked Pamela Hardacre more than he did in this moment. The look on Lady Goremore's face was priceless.

"You will not go upstairs!" Lady Goremore squawked, flapping her feathered arms at Pamela and Officer French, who was now talking to another two NWCU officers who'd appeared by the doors.

Lord Goremore was watching events with a stunned goggle-eyed expression. Jones whispered something in his ear and offered him a supportive arm. Lord Goremore rose and staggered out of the room clutching an empty wine glass.

It was dawning on Peaky and Madden that Jack wasn't actually dead and whilst they didn't understand how this could be possible, they had clearly worked out that they were in big trouble. Whilst everyone was watching Pamela and Lady Goremore, they made a break for it, sprinting towards a pair of French windows at the far end of the hall that opened out into the garden.

Jack heard a war cry and saw Vernon throw himself across two tables, hurtling into them, knocking them to the ground. Using a move that Jack assumed Vernon must've copied from WWE, he body dropped on top of both of them, his fists flying.

Constable Greenwood hurried over with handcuffs, calling for back-up through the radio on his lapel. He quickly put an end to the fight, much to Vernon's disappointment. "Ever thought of joining the Junior Police Cadets?" he asked Vernon as he handcuffed Peaky and Madden together. "I think you'd enjoy it."

"Jack! You did it!" Tara said, rushing forward with Terry and Tippi. "Peaky and Madden confessed in front of hundreds of witnesses!"

"This isn't over until Nick Skinner is behind bars and the lammergeier is safe," Jack said, jumping down from the table.

"Jack," Officer French called to him. "Would you take us up to the room you described to Constable Greenwood?"

"Terry, you take them," Jack said. "I need to get to

Passerine Pike." He hurried past Lady Goremore who was being read her rights. He saw his parents rise from their seats.

"Jack!" his mum called out. "I'm not sure what just happened. Are you all right?"

"Totally fine," Jack smiled brightly at them. "Can't stop. I'll explain later. I'm still helping the police."

"You do what you need to, son," his dad called out proudly after him.

"We need to get to Passerine Pike immediately," Jack cried as he reached Constable Greenwood's side. "Twitch, Ava and Ozuru are up there, trying to protect the lammergeier from Nick Skinner."

"A unit will be arriving any minute," Constable Greenwood replied, nodding to show he understood. "Let's get these two outside and round the front."

Constable Greenwood, flanked by Jack and Vernon, escorted Peaky and Madden out through the French doors and round to the driveway, just as three squad cars drove up, their blue lights flashing.

A sullen Peaky and Madden got into the back seat of the first squad car whilst Constable Greenwood gave instructions to the officers to take them back to the station. Then he turned to Jack. "Right, let's go. That's my car over there."

"I'm coming too," Vernon said, following Jack over to the silver car.

"Thanks," Jack replied, opening the door and getting into the passenger seat as Constable Greenwood slid into the driving seat and turned the key in the ignition.

Venon was scrambling into the back seat when they all heard Pamela shriek, "WAIT FOR US!" She was running down the steps of Mord Hall. Clem was right behind her with the camera.

Vernon held the door open, and a second later Pamela and Clem had jumped inside.

Jack glanced at Constable Greenwood, who looked like he was going to protest, but instead, he slammed his foot on the accelerator. "There's no time to argue," he said to everyone in the car, as he drove away from Mord Hall. "But when we get there, I don't want anyone trying to be a hero. We're talking about a man with a gun, and he knows how to use it."

"Yes, sir," they all mumbled meekly.

"You will all do *exactly* as I say, do you understand?"

"Yes, sir."

He reached down as his electric window opened. He slammed something onto the roof of his car, and Jack heard the wail of a siren as they raced up the road towards Passerine Pike.

Constable Greenwood's expression was deadly serious. Pamela was delivering an excited monologue to camera in the back. To Jack's delight, when they reached the car park, Constable Greenwood didn't stop. He drove onto the grass and up the hill. As they approached the Pike, a strange sight greeted them. Constable Greenwood stopped the car and shut off the lights.

Spread out, facing the Mord Estate were about sixty people standing, two metres apart, in a semi-circle. They each held a torch, or two torches, in their hands and they were using them as search spotlights, sweeping them along the fence, across the Mord Estate, into trees. Some of the beams of light seemed to wander randomly across the skyline.

"What are they doing?" Pamela asked.

"I think…" Jack said, staring at them. "I think Twitch is trying to make it impossible for Nick Skinner to get his sights on the bird by shining lots of lights in different directions. He's trying to blind him."

"Clever kid," Constable Greenwood said, sounding impressed. "Right, you lot, wait here one second. I just need to get something out of the boot." Slamming the door behind him, he walked to the boot, opened it, took out something, shut it, and then all the car locks popped down, trapping the four of them inside the car.

Constable Greenwood was already running up the hill. He didn't look back. Jack saw that he was armed.

"I don't believe this!" Pamela cried out. "Did he just lock us in the car! He can't do this! It was you who solved this case, Jack. He's treating us like children."

"Shh," Jack's eyes were locked on the policeman, as he waved a hand at Pamela. "We *are* children. There's an award-winning marksman out there. Constable Greenwood must have known we'd all try to come to Passerine Pike. Only way to make sure we were safe was to bring us himself and lock us in his car. He's smart, if you ask me." He shook his head. "I'm more worried about Twitch, Ava, Ozuru and the lammergeier. They're all out there and in the line of fire."

Pamela clambered into the front seat and all four of them peered out the car windows, trying to see their friends.

The roving spotlights were dizzying. Jack couldn't see the bearded vulture or make out who anyone was. There were a few torches that were held lower than the rest, and he guessed that a couple of them must be his friends.

Then he realized he'd lost sight of Constable Greenwood. His heart was thudding loudly. Everyone in the car was silent, even Pamela.

A minute later, all the torch beams went wild, dancing around like crazy.

"What's going on?" Pamela said, voicing the question in all of their minds.

On some silent command, all of the torch beams suddenly pointed at exactly the same spot. Jack gasped. Nick Skinner was lying flat on the rungs of a wooden ladder suspended along the top of the fence that bordered the Mord Estate. He held a shotgun in his arms, the wooden butt against his shoulder, his eye to the sight. He was lit up brightly by sixty torches.

They heard a shout, and Jack saw Constable Greenwood marching towards the gamekeeper with his gun in front of him.

"What's he saying?" Pamela strained to hear.

Jack stared at the constable's lips. "He's reading Nick Skinner his rights."

"You can read lips?" Pamela was impressed.

"My big brother's deaf," Jack replied. "I've signed and read lips for as long as I can remember."

"More cops!" Vernon announced as two more police cars, both off-road vehicles, drove past them.

Jack saw Twitch, Ava and Ozuru running down the hill towards him. The locks popped up and Jack flew out of the car.

"It's safe!" Twitch shouted. "The lammergeier is safe!"

"All the birdwatchers helped us!" Ozuru looked amazed.

"Nick Skinner's been arrested!" Ava whooped.

And suddenly Jack was jumping around with them, hugging his friends, and punching the air, riding high on victory and relief.

35
BIRDS OF A FEATHER

Jack knocked on Twitch's front door. He could hear music, chatter and approaching footsteps. It had been less than thirty-six hours since the Halloween Ball and he was still giddy from their victory.

"Jack! Come in." Iris, Twitch's mum, greeted him warmly as she opened the door. "The party's just getting started. We're all in the kitchen. Twitch has got some news he's waiting to share. He didn't want to tell anyone until you got here."

Jack followed her down the hall. Tara, Ozuru and Terry were seated around the kitchen table with Twitch. There were bowls of crisps and a plate of vegetarian sandwiches laid out under a *HAPPY BIRTHDAY* banner.

Twitch jumped up when he saw Jack.

"Happy birthday," Jack said, handing Twitch his gift. "I hope you like it."

Twitch tore off the paper and saw the large hardback book Jack had ordered especially for him. He read the title out, "*Birds of Paradise: Revealing the World's Most Extraordinary Birds!*" He looked at Jack in delight. "You remembered! From the conversation we had way back in the summer!" He hugged the book. "Thank you." He opened it and flicked through the pages.

"It's got pictures of all thirty-nine species in New Guinea," Jack said. "I remember you saying you'd like to go and see the birds of paradise. Maybe one day we'll go there together."

"I'd like that," Twitch said. "I've got a present for you too."

"It's not my birthday till May!" Jack protested.

"It's not wrapped." Twitch handed Jack an A4 envelope.

Opening the envelope, Jack slid out a photographic print of the lammergeier. It was one of the photos Twitch had taken when the boys had been hiding in the grass, watching the vulture. He drew in a tiny gasp, feeling the tingle of wonder in his chest all over again. "Thank you. I'm going to get this framed and hang it on my bedroom wall. It's so cool!"

The two boys exchanged a look. A moment of shared memory. Lifer and Spark.

"I've got news," Twitch said. "The BBC said my pictures of the lammergeier were the best ones they've seen of the bird. They're using them on the news website. They even paid me! I'm a professional nature photographer!" He looked overjoyed.

"That is so brilliant!" Jack exclaimed and the others congratulated him.

Iris ran to answer the door and returned with Ava, Tippi and Nan.

"Can I visit the chickens?" Tippi asked immediately.

"This is a birthday party," Ava said.

"Chickens like parties," Tippi insisted.

Iris ran to answer the door again, delighted that the house was filling with people. Jack was surprised to see Pamela, Vernon and Clem coming down the hall.

"What are you doing here?" Terry asked as they filed into the crowded kitchen.

"Hey! The Twitchers solved the mystery of who shot Splatty," Pamela protested. "I owe you guys. You've also made me a YouTube sensation." She beamed. "The video's had nearly a million views. I've decided I'm going to be a reporter on proper TV one day."

Jack thought this was a perfect job for Pamela.

"Ask them, Pamela," Vernon said.

"Ask us what?" Jack replied.

"Look, we're not saying we want to join the Twitchers, but…" Pamela swung her wrist in a circle to take in Vernon and Clem. "We were wondering whether we could be honorary members?" She batted her eyelashes at Jack.

"What does that mean?" Terry frowned. "Honorary members?"

"It means, we're interested in the crime-solving bit, but not the birdwatching bit."

"I've signed up to be a Junior Volunteer Police Cadet," Vernon said. "I'll be able to make citizen's arrests soon."

"I don't want to solve crimes really," Pamela said. "I just want to report on them."

"I'm training to be Pammy's cameraman," Clem said, blushing.

"We still think that looking at birds is boring," Pamela said. "But we get that you all like to do it and the world needs nerds who love nature. You're the good guys."

"You're not going to tease us any more?" Ozuru asked.

"A leopard can't change its spots," Terry said.

"I'll try to be nicer," Pamela said, sounding insincere. "I really will."

"What do you think, Jack?" Twitch looked at him.

"We made a pretty good team at Halloween." Jack shrugged. "And you never know, one day, Pamela might find her spark bird."

Twitch laughed. "Welcome, honorary members of the Twitchers."

"What's a spark bird?" Pamela asked. "Is it magic or something? Like a phoenix? Phoenixes aren't real, are they? Twitch, are phoenixes real?"

The Twitchers stifled their laughter and Pamela blushed.

"Did you hear about Lady Goremore?" she said, changing the subject. "She's in big trouble. Apparently, none of the birds in her private collection was licensed or registered, and lots of them are protected species. And, get this, I've got a contact on the inside that says all the money raised from ticket sales – the money that is supposed to go to a children's charity... She keeps most of it, she says to cover the cost of the party. She only donates a tiny percentage, but no way it costs that much... She's a thief!"

"No!" Tara was horrified.

"What happened to Peaky and Madden?" Jack asked. "I've not seen them." He'd been dreading bumping into the two bullies.

"My dad said their parents are furious," Pamela

replied. "They've had enough of their bad behaviour. They're talking about enlisting them in the army to teach them discipline." Pamela was enjoying being the centre of attention and dishing the dirt. "And did you hear about Nick Skinner?"

"No?" Jack leaned forward. "What?"

"He's been charged and is facing prison. When they went to his cottage, they found a taxidermy lab and photographs of the birds he's killed and stuffed. Apparently, he refused to say one word when he was taken to the police station. He won't speak to anybody."

Jack shuddered at the thought of the surly gamekeeper. "I'm glad he's being charged. I hope he goes to prison. He put Peaky and Madden up to the rabbit baiting and I'll bet he killed half the birds in Lady Goremore's collection."

"Pammy, give Twitch his birthday present." Clem handed her a badly wrapped gift.

"Oh, yes." Pamela dumped it into Twitch's hands. "Happy birthday from us. It seems a bit weird to me, but Tara told me you like these."

Twitch pulled off the paper.

"It's a teapot!" Jack gave Pamela an approving look.

"It's brand new," Twitch said, turning the sunny yellow teapot around in his hands. "I normally only hang broken ones in my tree."

"I'll break it for you if you like?" Vernon volunteered.

The doorbell went again, and Iris hurried to answer it. When she returned, she was following behind Twitch's next-door neighbour, Amita, who was carrying an enormous chocolate cake with fizzing sparklers on the top.

The adults broke out into song: "Happy birthday to you. Happy birthday to you."

"Happy bird-day dear Twitch," Jack sang raucously.

"HAPPY BIRD-DAY TO YOU!" everyone joined in.

"Guys, guys," Pamela called out. "I need all the Twitchers together please; my viewers want to meet you."

Clem got up and turned the phone video camera on them all.

Pamela sat herself between Jack and Twitch. "Meet Jack" – she gestured to him – "when he's not dressed as a zombie, or protecting vultures, he's the lead detective of the gang."

Jack beamed at this description.

"This is Twitch. He's the bird guru. He knows everything there is to know about birds. He formed the Twitchers to defeat a bank robber! Check my channel for the video about that crime. Hashtag Robber Ryan."

"Ava, Tippi." Pamela waved them over and turned to the camera. "Meet the *Kingfisher* sisters. Athlete" – she pointed at Ava, then at Tippi – "and artist."

"And this is Tara, one of my best friends," Pamela said, putting an arm around Tara's shoulder. Tara looked at her quizzically. "She's clever, loyal and knows a lot about gardening. I call her the Botanist."

Twitch stifled a laugh as Tara's eyebrows shot up.

"Ozuru loves to fish," Pamela went on, "for bad guys, and he's caught quite a few."

Ozuru mimed casting a fishing rod, then gave the camera a thumbs up.

"And of course, I am your favourite roving reporter…"

"Hey!" Terry exclaimed. "What about me!"

"How could I forget?" Pamela laughed. "Terry is our Dr Watson." She leaned her head on his shoulder affectionately. "He's everyone's favourite. He's the brother you love to tease, but he'll be there for you, even if you've been horrid to him."

"And I'm the muscle!" Vernon declared, coming up behind them and doing an Incredible Hulk roar.

"You've been watching Pamela Hardacre, and her cute cameraman Clem. See you all soon, and remember, if you've got a crime that needs solving, you need: the Twitchers."

Jack looked at Twitch and they both grinned.

AUTHOR'S NOTES AND ACKNOWLEDGEMENTS

In July 2020, when I was putting the final touches to *Twitch*, a bearded vulture was spotted in the skies over the United Kingdom, for only the second time in recorded history. It caused great excitement on the social media feeds of the birders I follow. I had never heard of a lammergeier. I looked it up and discovered a misunderstood bird on the brink of extinction, with so much character and cultural resonance in other parts of the world. I was immediately fascinated. To my delight, one of the young birders who were the inspiration for the Twitchers, Indy Kiemel Greene, not only got to see the bearded vulture in the Derbyshire Peaks, but he photographed it and his images were used widely. That ornithological event was the spark for this story.

If *Twitch* is the origin story of the Twitchers, my gang of birdwatching detectives, then this book is about Jack becoming a birder. It reflects my own desires and struggles with being a birdwatcher and feeling I belong. My spark bird was a kingfisher. I saw it in 2019 in the

Cromwell Bottom Nature Reserve, which Aves Wood is based upon. Seeing that bird has changed the way I view the world and opened my mind to birdwatching.

If you haven't seen your spark bird yet, don't worry – there is one out there waiting for you, you just have to keep a look out.

I would like to thank Paddy Donnelly who has, yet again, produced beautiful artwork for the cover of this book. I am grateful to everyone at Walker Books, for launching *Twitch* into the skies at such a tricky time and ensuring it flew into readers' hands, where, to my delight, it has been much loved. Thank you, Denise Johnstone-Burt and Megan Middleton, my excellent (and patient) editors, as well as Kirsten, Ellen, Ben, Ed and everyone at Walker Books who played a part in helping me make this book.

I'm grateful for the tireless work and support of my husband, Sam Harmsworth Sparling, and my indomitable agent, Kirsty McLachlan of Morgan Green Creatives, as well as the love and understanding from my boys, Arthur and Sebastian, whose lives I ceaselessly mine for inspiration.

And to every birder, reader, reviewer, bookseller, librarian and teacher who has picked up this book and read it all the way to this very last sentence, thank you too.

Maya x

Discover the Twitchers' first mystery adventure!

Twitch has three pet chickens, four pigeons, swallows nesting in his bedroom and a passion for birdwatching. On the first day of the summer holidays, he arrives at his secret hide to find police everywhere. A convicted robber has broken out of prison and is hiding in Aves Wood. Can Twitch use his talents for birdwatching in the hunt for the dangerous prisoner and find the missing loot?

**WINNER OF THE CRIMEFEST AWARD FOR
BEST CRIME NOVEL FOR CHILDREN 2021**

WINNER OF THE SAINSBURY'S CHILDREN'S BOOK AWARDS 2021

Available from all good booksellers!

M. G. LEONARD is an award-winning, bestselling writer of children's books, as well as a member of Authors4Oceans. Her books are sold in 40 countries, and there is currently a TV series in development based on her Beetle Boy series. Her first picture book, *The Tale of a Toothbrush*, is out now. She is also co-author of the critically acclaimed Adventures on Trains series, and the author of The Twitchers, a mystery adventure series starring a group of birdwatching detectives. Before becoming a writer, M. G. Leonard worked as a digital media producer for the National Theatre, The Royal Opera House and Shakespeare's Globe. She lives in Brighton with her husband, two sons and pet beetles.

#TheTwitchers
@WalkerBooksUK
@MGLnrd